CADE

and the
BURGLED BLIZZARD-BRISTLES

and the
BURGLED BLIZZARD-BRISTLES

Peter Nelson & Rohitash Rao

Balzer + Bray
An Imprint of HarperCollins*Publishers*

Balzer + Bray is an imprint of HarperCollins Publishers.

Creature Keepers and the Burgled Blizzard-Bristles
Copyright © 2016 by Peter Nelson and Rohitash Rao
All rights reserved. Printed in the United States of America.
No part of this book may be used or reproduced in any manner
whatsoever without written permission except in the case of
brief quotations embodied in critical articles and reviews. For
information address HarperCollins Children's Books, a division
of HarperCollins Publishers, 195 Broadway, New York, NY 10007.
www.harpercollinschildrens.com

Library of Congress Control Number: 2016941522
ISBN 978-0-06-223647-0

Typography by Alison Klapthor
16 17 18 19 20   CG/RRDH   10 9 8 7 6 5 4 3 2 1

First Edition

*To my brother Sean, who found himself
on the mountaintop, then found the strength
to come back down—P. N.*

*To my amazing, wonderful sister-in-law, Natalia,
thank you for keeping our family so strong
(Oh, and tell your daughter to put down
Percy Jackson and start reading this!)—R. R.*

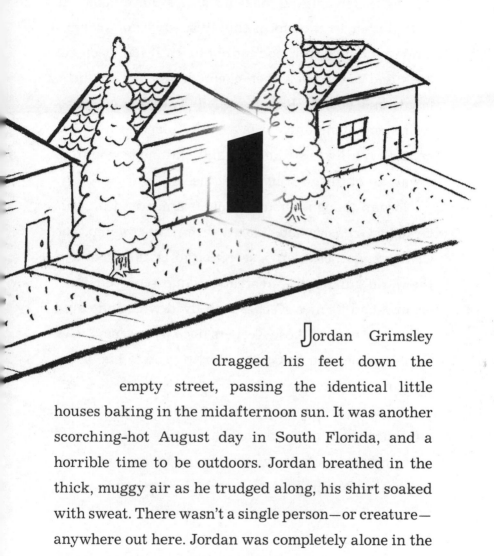

Jordan Grimsley dragged his feet down the empty street, passing the identical little houses baking in the midafternoon sun. It was another scorching-hot August day in South Florida, and a horrible time to be outdoors. Jordan breathed in the thick, muggy air as he trudged along, his shirt soaked with sweat. There wasn't a single person—or creature— anywhere out here. Jordan was completely alone in the middle of a full-blown heat wave.

Jordan enjoyed these walks. The soupy air of the Okeeyuckachokee Swamp that hung heavy over his little dead-end street helped him to think. On this day, he was imagining the work it must have taken his grandfather to transform this little sliver of swampland into a neighborhood for old folks. It had been cut back and paved over, then covered with perfect little lawns and houses. Jordan smiled. The Eternal Acres retirement community was a lovely place to live. But beneath it all was still a wild and untamed swamp. In a way, all of this was just a disguise.

Jordan thought about the other amazing thing his Grampa Grimsley had created within this swamp. The Creature Keepers were a secret organization that kept the world's undiscovered creatures undiscovered. Each cryptid had its own Keeper who lived with and cared for it. And each of those Keepers lived by a solemn vow: to help, hide, and hoax, in order to protect his or her creature.

As a young man traveling the world, George Grimsley had come across his very first cryptid quite by accident. He was lucky enough to have his camera with him, and he was luckier still to snap a picture of the strange beast. Hoping for wealth and fame, young George Grimsley sold the photograph, exposing that creature to the world. The Chupacabra, as it became known, was feared and despised by the people of North America, and soon chased and hunted all over the world. George Grimsley grew to regret what he had done to this innocent creature. He realized Chupacabra would have been better left undiscovered. And so he made it his life's work to hide and protect as many cryptids as he could find. All accepted his help but one—the Chupacabra never forgave George Grimsley.

Standing alone on the steamy sidewalk, Jordan wondered not for the first time how his grandfather could have possibly done all of this on his own. In less than a year, Jordan and his sister had met the Loch Ness Monster, the Sasquatch, the Giant Desert Jackalope, and the Brazilian Mapinguari, just to name a few.

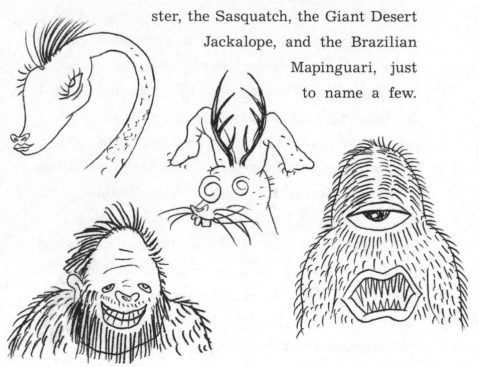

All of these cryptids and many more had been tracked down by his Grampa Grimsley, then befriended and persuaded to accept the protection of the Creature Keepers. Jordan knew some of these creatures personally. They could be quite stubborn. So how did his grandfather do this all by himself?

As the blazing sun scorched his face, a cold realization sank in—there was a lot Jordan didn't know about his grandfather, and that wasn't likely to change. His Grampa Grimsley had met a terrible fate in this very swamp, in the form of a very large and very hungry alligator. All of his research and his many journals were lost in a massive flood that destroyed the original Creature Keeper lair deep in the Okeeyuckachokee, a flood that Jordan himself had had a hand in, and still felt quite awful about. The only thing left behind was a single journal of Grampa Grimsley's, which Jordan kept with him at all times. He'd read it backward and forward. Unfortunately, it posed more questions about his grandfather's mysterious life than it answered.

Jordan closed his eyes. The late summer air was like a fluffy blanket, muffling the sounds around him—the chirps of a bird overhead, the purr of a lawnmower down the block, a droning baseball game from a television inside one of the houses across the street.

Skreeeee!

A sound squealed inside his ear, startling him. It was followed by a voice he found equally irritating—that of his sister, Abbie.

"Yo, dorkface. Where are you? They're ready for us. Get back here." The tiny transmitter inside Jordan's ear squealed again, then went silent. Jordan looked down the dead-end street. Sitting grandly where the perfect little lawns of Eternal Acres ended and the wild Okeeyuckachokee Swamp began, the beautifully restored retirement home looked like a great dam holding back the vast, tangled wildness that stretched out for miles and miles beyond it. Jordan took another deep, cottony breath of the muggy air, then headed toward his Grampa Grimsley's enormous house.

An air-conditioned blast sent a raw chill straight through Jordan's damp shirt as he stepped inside. He passed the living room, nodding to the wrinkly old residents—all current or former Creature Keepers—sitting around sipping lemonade, playing cards, and watching television. Each one of them wore hearing aids very similar to the transmitter in Jordan's ear, and they all returned his nods with disapproving glares. Jordan kept moving but spoke softly out of the side of his mouth.

"Okay, okay, I'm heading down now." His voice
crackled inside the ear of each of the old-timers staring
at him. "You can all stop giving me the stink eye and
instead maybe give me a position on Poppa Bear and
Momma Bea—"

"Well, there you are!" Jordan's mother bellowed with delight as she stepped out in front of
him. Throughout the living room, the elderly retired
Keepers all yanked out their transmitters as Mrs.
Grimsley's voice squealed in their ears. She'd emerged
from one of the many bedrooms that lined the long
hallway with a big grin on her face. Jordan heard
an old man's voice whisper in his earpiece, "Momma
Bear, twelve o'clock."

"Yes, I can see that!" Jordan hollered back toward the living room.

Mrs. Grimsley glanced around. "See what, sweetie? Are you feeling all right?"

Jordan's mother was a slightly messy woman, especially when she was in her fixer-upper mode, which was nearly always. Today she wore an apron and a pair of bright yellow rubber gloves. She pulled one glove off with a snap and felt Jordan's sweaty brow. "You must be delirious. You've been walking around in this beastly weather again, haven't you? Your father's looking for you with his clipboard of to-do's. Did you replace the batteries in Mrs. Rooney's hearing aid like he asked?"

"Did it this morning, Mom."

"Thank you." She smiled at him. "It's so wonderful how my adorable little Einstein invented those clever hearing aids for all of our residents!" She thought for a second. "Although it was strange how everyone's hearing seemed to go at the same time. . . ."

"Yeah, well. You know old people. Stuff just starts going wrong all over the place. Probably why they get so grumpy—and impatient."

Skreeee! Jordan's earpiece suddenly rang in his ear, followed by whispers and grunts of disapproval. *"Speak for yourself, sonny!" "I'll show you what grumpy looks like, you whippersnapper!"*

Jordan smirked back at the scowling old folk, then peered down the long hallway. At the opposite end, his sister, Abbie, stood just inside the kitchen. She looked angry with him, which was nothing new. Jordan turned his attention back to his mother. "Mom, I need to do something now. In the kitchen. So—"

"Good!" She began following him. "I'll get you a cold pack for your head. I can't have my adorable little Einstein frying that cute little brain of his!"

An elderly woman suddenly leaped out of the next room and threw her arms up dramatically as she flopped at Mrs. Grimsley's feet. "Goodness gracious!" she cried. "I seem to have fallen and I don't even know why!"

Mrs. Grimsley bent down to help. "Mrs. Rooney! Are you all right?"

The old woman rolled around on the floor, but winked at Jordan as she gestured for him to keep moving down the hall. Jordan moved quickly away from his mother, straight for his sister, who was still waiting by the kitchen door.

"Nice of you to finally show up," Abbie said.

Even though Jordan was twelve and Abbie just two years older, she somehow always knew exactly the right thing to say to make him feel like a preschooler. "Go on," she said, opening the basement door and following him down the dark staircase. "You've made us late enough."

The Grimsley siblings walked straight past all the usual basementy stuff, up to a large, rusty old water heater in the corner. There was a keypad on it, and Jordan punched in a code. The metal shell of the water heater spun around, sliding open to reveal an empty chamber, just like an elevator car. In fact, it *was* an elevator car. Jordan and his sister stepped inside and the door slid closed behind them. They whooshed down, deep beneath the house, until the secret elevator came to a stop and the door slid open again.

Jordan and Abbie stepped into a large, bright, cavernous room buzzing with activity. Elderly people everywhere were busily manning computer terminals, studying charts, and reading digital maps. Every one of them wore an ill-fitting uniform and seemed to be doing very important work. A large screen on the far wall showed a map of the world with various dots at points around the globe. A group of elderly technicians stared intently at the dots on the map, discussing their movement and positions.

"Well, well," a voice boomed from the center of the floor. A plump old woman stepped forwarded holding a *#1 Boss* coffee mug in one hand and a stopwatch in the other. "Look who *finally* found his way to the Creature Keepers central command—our own adorable little Einstein!"

GLOBAL CRYPTID POSITIONING SYSTEM

The technicians giggled and snickered. They all wore the same earpieces as the undercover Keeper crew upstairs.

"Y'know," Jordan said, pulling the

tiny transmitter out of
his ear, "sometimes I wish
I hadn't invented these things."

Doris was anything but the typical little old lady in charge of an underground global command-and-support creature-protection center. She had a history with Grampa Grimsley and was probably the last person to see him alive. Because of this, she shared a special bond with Jordan. Of course, that bond didn't keep her from letting Jordan know when she wasn't pleased with him.

"You must have a load of bricks in your britches!" Doris shoved her stopwatch in Jordan's face. "You call that a response time? I've seen Ed move faster—and he's got seriously swollen bunions!"

Ed, a balding man with a *#2 Boss* coffee mug, leaned over and whispered to her. "Doris, I told you about my bunions in confidence."

Like the Keepers out in the field all over the world who lived with their creatures, Doris, Ed, and the rest of the Creature Keeper Command Center support crew were, until recently, very young—kept at Jordan's age by drinking an elixir derived from the Fountain of Youth. But that all came to a sudden and frightening halt when an enemy of the Creature Keepers, Señor Areck Gusto, cruelly exposed them to the Puddle of Ripeness—a particularly nasty swamp substance that immediately reversed the elixir's effects, painfully returning them to their proper ages. This unfortunate event was also partly Jordan's fault. Which was another thing he still felt awful about.

"Blame Jordan," Abbie said, nodding toward her brother. "He's the reason we were late getting down here. He was on one of his heat-wave walkabouts again."

Jordan ignored them both and pointed at the great blinking map on the back wall. "How's the search going, Doris? Any sign of that slimy goatsucker?"

Jordan was referring to Chupacabra, his long lost grandfather's archenemy. Not only had the evil cryptid recently resurfaced, but Jordan had made a shocking discovery the last time they met, when it was revealed that Chupacabra and Señor Areck Gusto were one and the same.

Disguised as Gusto, Chupacabra had been able to maneuver back and forth between the cryptid and human worlds. He was responsible for flooding the Creature Keepers' underground lair and destroying the Fountain of Youth elixir that kept the Keepers young. But worst of all, he'd managed to steal the powers from two of the three most special cryptids under the Creature Keepers' protection.

Of all the cryptids known to the Creature Keepers, there were three who each possessed a sacred, elemental power—and Chupacabra had found a way to tap into not just one, but two of them. First he hatched a successful plot to kidnap the Loch Ness Monster. Once she was captured, he cruelly hijacked her water-controlling Hydro-Hide. Soon after, he pulled off an equally diabolical scheme to steal Syd the Sasquatch's Soil-Soles, snatching for himself the power to manipulate earth and split solid rock.

Thanks to Jordan and Abbie, the CKCC was able to rescue Nessie. And while she had lost her Hydro-Hide to Chupacabra, she had begun to grow back her coat of extraordinary scales—and with it, her control over the world's lakes and oceans. Jordan and Abbie were also successful in reclaiming one of Syd's two Soil-Soles. This was shortly before they torched Chupacabra with a massive jet thruster, blasting his charred body clear across the Great White North—which Jordan did not feel awful about in the least.

Doris turned back to the big map on the wall. The Global Cryptid Positioning System, or GCPS, was Jordan's greatest contribution to the command center. Electronic devices were distributed to each and every cryptid under Creature Keeper protection. These tracking bracelets were worn on ankles, tails, claws, fins—wherever they could be attached. Once installed and activated, each one emitted a signal that showed up on the big map. From inside the secret bunker beneath Eternal Acres, Doris and her crew could track any cryptid's whereabouts, anywhere in the world.

Chupacabra had unknowingly swallowed one of the tracking bracelets before being blasted across the sky. But mysteriously, almost immediately after being violently jettisoned toward the Arctic Circle, the signal had gone dead.

Doris pointed to a dim light on the map, near the center of Asia. "This can't be right, but we have picked up a very faint signal coming from the barren Xinjiang territory of China, just south of the Gobi Desert."

"No way Chupacabra is still alive," Abbie said. "We flash-fried that corn dog. Must be a glitch in your software, Einstein."

Jordan peered up at the dim light on the map. He

knew his tracking technology was glitch-free. But Abbie and Doris were right. Even Chupacabra couldn't have survived a blast like that. Even if he had, Jordan found it hard to believe that Chupacabra could then make his way from wherever he crash-landed in northern Canada all the way to the no-man's-land of central China.

SMASH! A far wall suddenly crumbled as a pair of gigantic antlers broke through from the other side. A large, dazed-looking Desert Jackalope poked its fluffy bunny head into the chamber and stood there panting like an oversized Labradoodle.

Then again, Jordan suddenly remembered, next to impossible seemed to happen a lot since he'd become an honorary Creature Keeper.

Riding atop Peggy was a kid in a crisp uniform that included a well-ironed sash festooned with tiny, sewn-on merit patches. "Great job, Peggy," he said, sliding off her back. "That new addition will make a great snack lounge. Maybe my alter ego, C. E. Noodlepen, can release a little more of George Grimsley's savings to spring for a Ping-Pong table!" He patted Peggy on the nose. "Take a carrot break, girl. You earned it."

Peggy curled up in a corner as the boy approached the others. "Sorry I'm late, everyone," he said, straightening his bolo tie and adjusting his hat.

Eldon Pecone was a First-Class Badger Ranger and Chief Creature Keeper. Jordan's grandfather had left him in charge, along with a small inheritance that he could access under the guise of fake-lawyer C. E. Noodlepen. With Mr. Noodlepen's financial help, Jordan's technological know-how, and Doris overseeing every detail, Creature Keeper Command Center was finally operating as if it were in the twenty-first century. Eldon was happy for all the changes, but didn't understand any of it. He'd earned Badger Badges for everything from Aardvark Trapping to Zinc Mining. But he couldn't tell a hard drive from a hatbox.

Eldon pointed to the digital map on the wall. "So if I'm to understand correctly, that blinky thingy on that electrical wall map represents one of Jordan's tracking doohickeys, which was last known to be inside of Chupacabra's belly."

"That's right, dearie," Doris said. "More or less."

"So since it's popped up again, that means Jordan's whatchamajiggy survived."

"And moved," Abbie added. "About three thousand miles."

"Not by itself," Jordan said. They all exchanged worried glances. "Doris, has the signal moved since it popped up in China?"

Ed spoke up. "Negative. We've been watching it very closely. It reappeared and hasn't moved an inch."

Abbie let out a sigh. "Okay," she said. "See? Chupacabra's gotta be dead. He crashed and burned up in the Arctic somewhere."

"Why didn't we pick up a signal where he crashed?" Jordan asked.

"Landed on his belly," she said. "Or whatever was left of it. Blocked the signal."

"How'd the tracker get to China?"

"Easy. Some large seabird swooped by, picked herself up a charred chunk of Chupa, flew southwest, and dropped it. Tracker popped out, provided a signal that showed up on our map. Mystery solved. Chupacabra dead."

"Ew," Ed said. He looked a bit pale.

Jordan turned to Eldon. "Any thoughts on my sister's theory?"

"Pile of poop," Eldon said.

"Excuse me?" Abbie spat.

Eldon pulled out and presented a long-handled tool with an open-mouthed scraper at the end. "Pile of poop! That's *my* theory."

"Wait," Abbie said. "What is that? Because it looks a lot like a—"

"It's a T-549," Ed said. "Standard-issue midsized cryptid pooper-scooper."

"And what the heck is it for?" Abbie said.

"Scooping poop, dearie." Doris smiled. "Another mystery solved."

Jordan looked from the pooper-scooper to Eldon. "So if Abbie's right, my tracker is still inside Chupacabra's dead, decaying carcass. But if you're right, it's—"

"It's not," Eldon said. "Because he pooped it out."

"Which would mean he could still be alive." Jordan swallowed. "And . . . he could be anywhere."

"No way," Abbie said again. "I saw that thruster incinerate that creep."

"Well, there's only one way to know for sure," Eldon

said. "Our Elite Keepers need to go and check it out." He shoved the T-549 standard-issue midsized cryptid pooper-scooper into Abbie's hand. She shoved it back at him.

"No, no," she said. "This isn't what I signed on for."

"Eldon's right," Jordan said. "We have to confirm that Chupacabra's dead. And if he isn't—" Jordan looked down at the shiny gold CK badge that Eldon had given him and his sister when they were officially promoted to Elite Keepers. He took the T-549 from Eldon and held it up proudly. "Abbie, this is a high-priority, top secret recon operation. And it's exactly what we signed on for."

TODAY'S THE
GREATEST
DAY
EVER
!

"Fine, I'll go. But let's not kid ourselves. We're being sent to clean up doo-doo."

Jordan smiled at his sister. She smirked back at him. "But I'm pretty sure your first priority, little Einstein, is to invent an explanation for Mom and Dad as to why we're suddenly flying off to China."

Ding-dong! The upstairs doorbell rang over the CKCC loudspeakers.

Eldon smiled slyly. "Sounds like someone's at the door. Maybe you two had better go upstairs and see who it is."

3

Jordan and Abbie snuck back up the basement stairs, cut through the kitchen, and made their way down the long hallway toward the front door of the house. As they approached, they could see their mother welcoming someone with big hugs and cheery greetings. Their father bowed robotically, as if he were doing some weird ab-crunching workout. He turned when he saw them coming. "There you are! Jordan! Abbie! Come meet your replacements!"

Jordan and Abbie looked at each other as Mr. and Mrs. Grimsley stepped aside. Standing in the doorway, dressed in Badger Ranger uniforms, were a girl and a boy, about sixteen, both with similar features. Very similar features.

"They're twins!" Mrs. Grimsley blurted out. "All the way from Japan! This is Katsu and Shika . . . *Ashooky*? Am I pronouncing that correctly?"

"*Asukoh*," said the boy, Katsu. He bowed while staring at them intensely. Jordan had read somewhere that in Japanese culture this was considered an insult. And he got the distinct feeling that this was exactly Katsu's intention. The girl, Shika, seemed friendlier. She glanced downward as she bowed, revealing a tiny turtle backpack on her back. Then she rose back up, smiling apologetically.

"Asukoh, yes," Mrs. Grimsley said. "Please forgive me."

"Katsu and Shika are part of the Badger Ranger Exchanger Program," Mr. Grimsley said. "They're here to be exchanged with you! Isn't that something?"

Jordan and Abbie were equally confused. Shika noticed. She stepped forward and winked at them. "You know, the exchange program. *Master Ranger Bernie* is parking the car. He will explain and help you to understand, I am sure."

CRASH! Outside, a small red convertible sports car was crunched up against the front gate. Behind the wheel was Bernard—a very large, very poorly disguised Skunk Ape, wrestling with an inflated air bag that had shot out of the steering wheel. He gave a thumbs-up to everyone.

"I'm okay!" he called out.

Bernard lived in the Okeeyuckachokee Swamp and was the first cryptid Jordan had ever met. Eldon was technically his Keeper, although Jordan had often wondered who really took care of whom. Bernard was very independent-minded, and quite sophisticated for a cryptid. He enjoyed doing lots of human-type things, from scuba diving to playing the tuba. He especially loved operating large, fast, and potentially dangerous vehicles. He also seemed to leap at any chance to shave off as much of his thick, smelly black fur as he could, stuff his oversized body into one of Eldon's old Badger Ranger uniforms, and pretend to be a human.

"Ranger Master Bernie!" Mrs. Grimsley greeted the patchily shaved Skunk Ape lumbering up her walkway. "How lovely to see you again!"

"Hey there, big guy!" Mr. Grimsley briskly shook Bernard's thick paw-hand. "How're things in the great wilderness?"

"Great!" Bernard said. "Couldn't be more wilder-nessy, thank you." He turned to Abbie and Jordan, who were staring at his way-too-small khaki shorts. "So. I trust you Badger Ranger Exchanger Rangers are all, uh, Badger-ready to go?"

Jordan and Abbie looked at their parents. The proud grins on the faces of Mr. and Mrs. Grimsley told them all they needed to know.

They turned to the twins. Shika grinned at them oddly, then suddenly burst into tears. Katsu quickly put his arm around her and stiffly comforted her, while glaring at Jordan. "Please excuse my twin sister. She is emotional from our long journey, and a little homesick. But she will be fine."

The girl nodded and smiled through her tears. *HONK-HONK!* The red sports car diverted their attention outside again. Bernard had somehow run back down, pushed the car off the gate, and was back in the driver's seat, revving the engine and waving for them to hurry up.

Jordan and Abbie kissed their parents good-bye, tossed a few items in their backpacks, and a few minutes later were pulling away from their grandfather's house, Bernard behind the wheel. As Jordan and Abbie looked back, they could see their father already talking to the Badger Ranger Exchanger Rangers about home improvement.

"Those poor twins," Abbie said. "He's probably asking them what they know about bathroom grout removal."

Jordan turned to their stubbly-shaved chauffeur as he drove them out of the Eternal Acres development and turned onto the bumpy, pothole-filled Ingraham Highway. "Bernard, Katsu and Shika seem very nice, but we're needed in China, not Japan. You know there's a difference, right?"

"Please. I'm well-studied in all geography, including that of the eastern hemisphere." Bernard suddenly veered the little car off the road, straight into the thick, tangled swamp.

"How are you on the geography of where you're driving right now?" Abbie yelled as branches and vines slapped her and her brother in the face and head. Bernard jerked the wheel left and right to avoid crashing into the giant cypress trees or nose-diving into the muddy pools that dotted the Everglades.

"Where are we going?" Jordan hollered.

"Into the swamp," Bernard shouted back. "It's a secret way to the boathouse."

"I didn't know there was an access road into the boathouse from out here."

"There isn't! That's what makes it so secret!"

A minute later, Bernard fishtailed the car into a clearing deep within the swamp, bringing the wild ride to a sudden stop. He unbuckled his seat belt and hopped out. "Here we are!" Abbie and Jordan rolled out of the car onto the ground. Their faces were scratched and covered in mud, their hair tangled with twigs and branches.

"On your feet, Elite Keepers!" Eldon's voice called out from a hidden boathouse where the Okeeyucka-chokee met the shore of the bay. Inside was the Creature Keepers' modest collection of vehicles. Parked near the foot of a long dock was the Heli-Jet, a very slick and modern-looking chopper-airplane hybrid. Bernard began tossing their gear into the aircraft's side cargo door as Eldon stormed up to him. "What have I told you about driving in the daytime? Keep defying me and you'll be on your way to getting your privileges revoked, buster!"

Before Bernard could open his mouth to defend himself, a muffled, echoey, high-pitched scream was heard from a large cypress-tree stump nearby. A false top popped open like a hatch, releasing a whoosh of air, followed by the Asukoh twins. They came flying out of it, followed by Doris. The three of them tumbled onto the soft, mossy ground, rolling to a stop at Eldon's feet.

"Ha!" Doris laughed as she stood up. "That pneumatic transport tunnel connecting the boathouse and the command center was a marvelous addition, Jordan! And such a time-saver!"

Jordan helped Shika to her feet. "I should've designed it to be a little less terrifying," he said to her. "Don't feel bad. First time I tried it, I screamed, too." Shika giggled and shook her head. Then she gestured with her eyes at her twin brother, who was blushing and breathing heavily. "Oh." Jordan tried to give Katsu a hand, but he just glared at Jordan as he stood up on his own.

"Where are Mac and Nessie?" Jordan asked. "Aren't they coming with us?"

"The desert isn't ideal for Nessie or Mac, geographically speaking," Bernard said. He picked up Eldon's pack and threw it rather carelessly into the hull of the Heli-Jet. "On account of Nessie being a giant water cryptid, and the fact that Mac gets sunburned really easily."

Nessie, of course, was the Loch Ness Monster. Mac was Alistair MacAlister, her red-haired, pale-skinned Scottish Creature Keeper. They were both fun to have on an adventure, and Jordan had hoped they'd be coming along.

"And what about Kriss?" Abbie asked, trying to sound nonchalant. Kriss was the West Virginian Mothman, who was also very useful—not to mention shy, dark, and moody, traits that Abbie happened to admire very much.

"The three of them are out in the field," Doris added. "In addition to our little wandering tracker-collar mystery, the GCPS map has been showing a small breakout of wandering cryptids near the northern coast of the

Indian Ocean. We picked up their signals earlier, and are getting confirmation from local sources. The South African Grootslang was seen swimming up the coast of Madagascar. And the Australian Bunyip was spotted standing on a beach a bit north of Perth, just staring out over the water. Definitely weird, but nothing Kriss, Mac, and Nessie can't get to the bottom of."

"Let me get this straight," Abbie said. "You've got multiple cryptids doing Jordan's weirdo walkabouts, but you're sending us Elite Keepers to go poop-scooping in the middle of nowhere?"

"Mac, Nessie, and Kriss can return the cryptids home before anyone spots them," Eldon said. "I need you Elite Keepers to help me with a potentially far more dangerous situation—and to find out if the two are somehow related."

"Besides," Bernard said, "if they're having any trouble, we can help them out. We'll just be on the other side of the Himalayas."

"I just hope you fly a little more cautiously than you drive," Abbie said.

Eldon gave Bernard a disapproving look, and Bernard turned away in a huff to finish packing up the Heli-Jet.

"This is an all-hands-on-deck situation," Eldon said, looking at the Asukoh twins. "Katsu and Shika,

I know you've made sacrifices by coming here to help. And I promise you, Morris will remain safe in his inanimate state."

"Morris?" Jordan turned to Katsu. "Who's Morris?"

The boy grunted, crossed his arms, and turned away.

"Morris is our cryptid," Shika explained. "The Kappa. And we were asked to leave him all alone." Tears began to well in her eyes. She walked off toward the shoreline.

Jordan stepped closer to Katsu and held out his hand. "Hey, I didn't know you were a Keeper," he said, holding out his hand. "Me too. Well, sort of."

Katsu looked at Jordan's Elite Keeper badge. Then he looked down at Jordan's hand as if he were made of slimy snot. He sneered and turned away again.

Abbie watched this, then walked down to the water, where Shika was standing alone.

"Hey," Abbie said. "Your brother's not a very happy guy, is he?" Shika shook her head no. "I can totally relate to that," Abbie continued. "And I can only imagine how hard it must've been for you two to leave your creature all alone."

"Thank you, but that is not why Katsu is so angry," Shika said softly. "He doesn't think your brother is worthy to be a Creature Keeper. He considers your brother to be . . . a brainless toad."

Abbie glanced over at Katsu. "Your brother and I have a lot in common," she said.

Shika began to cry quietly. Abbie looked at her, unsure what to do. She awkwardly put her arm around the girl. "Uh—there, there. Don't do that. It'll be okay. I promise. Just, y'know, stop it."

Shika looked up and smiled with tears still in her eyes. "Will you see that Morris is safe? He is so help-less and alone. Please, promise me you will make sure he's okay when you are done collecting the Chupacabra droppings."

Abbie stared at Shika, then looked over at the Heli-Jet, where Eldon was handing Bernard the T-549 midsized cryptid pooper-scooper, as well as a box of industrial rubber gloves. She looked back at Shika.

"You have my word."

"Thank you!" Shika hugged Abbie. "I knew when I saw you we would be BFFs!"

"Okay. No need to hug," Abbie said stiffly. "And BFF really isn't what this is."

"C'mon, let's move out, Elite Keepers!" Eldon yelled to them from aboard the Heli-Jet as Bernard fired up the silent rotors from inside the cockpit.

Abbie wriggled free from Shika, who frantically rummaged through her turtle backpack. "Wait," she said, handing Abbie a book. "This is for you. Just in case."

"Abbie!" Jordan called out as he was boarding the Heli-Jet. "Let's go!"

Abbie ran and jumped aboard the Heli-Jet just as Eldon was sliding the door shut. She buckled in as they began to lift away from the swamp, and peered out the window at the people on the ground below. Doris waved. Katsu glared jealously. Shika was jumping up and down. Abbie looked at the book in her hands. It was titled, *Raising and Caring for Your Kappa*. She glanced around to make sure no one had seen it, then quickly slipped it into her backpack.

4

The Heli-Jet cleared the knotty tree line of the Okeeyuckachokee Swamp and hovered there for a second as Bernard ignited its massive jet engines. Then it blasted across the sky. Jordan sunk back in his seat and felt the power of the rockets, thinking to himself that there's no way they couldn't have incinerated the Chupacabra to ashes. He pulled out his mobile GCPS tracker and checked the dot representing the tracking bracelet on the screen's map. It was still there, south of the Gobi Desert, pulsing faintly, motionless.

Jordan began flipping through his grandfather's old journal. There was something that had bothered Jordan since he first met Chupacabra, a feeling he could never put his finger on. Now with the possibility that the creature might be gone, Jordan was beginning to untangle what it might be. Chupacabra had never believed that Jordan's grandfather was dead. He even thought that Jordan himself was actually George Grimsley in disguise, just as so many Creature Keepers had been old people hiding in plain sight as their younger selves. Jordan knew that Chupacabra's hunger for revenge and his desire to kill his grandfather had something to do with this crazy idea. But Jordan also had an odd fear that there might be something else Chupacabra knew about his grandfather, something that Jordan might never learn if the creature was dead. As the Heli-Jet zoomed eastward on its overnight flight, Jordan drifted off to sleep, holding this thought in his head, and his grandfather's journal tightly in his arms.

"Apple juice?"

Jordan opened his eyes to see Bernard standing over him wearing a strange plastic hat. "We're over the Xinjiang territory," the Skunk Ape said. "We should be approaching the drop zone soon. It's all desert down there, so it's important to stay hydrated." Bernard's hat had a cup holder with an apple juice box on either side. Straws from each box curved down into the sides of the Skunk Ape's mouth. Spelled out in big block letters

35

across the hat were the words "THIRST AID."

"This is my hands-free beverage helmet," Bernard said proudly. "Allows me to enjoy refreshing beverages while keeping my paws on the controls. Cool, right?"

Before Jordan could answer, Eldon sat down next to Jordan and took an apple juice from his creature. "I don't know where you got that thing," he said. "But if you've been sneaking out again for shopping trips in that little car of yours, you're in big trouble, buddy-boy."

Bernard rolled his eyes and turned on his heel, marching back into the cockpit.

"You're being a little hard on him, don't you think?" Jordan said. They both watched as Bernard confidently hopped into the pilot's seat and sipped from his hands-free beverage helmet. "I mean, what are you so protective about? He's such a responsible guy."

"He's not a *guy*," Eldon said. "He's a cryptid. My cryptid. And yes, while he knows a lot about the human world, that's exactly the kind of curiosity that killed the Skunk Ape."

Abbie woke and stretched. "Where are we?" she asked.

"We're close," Jordan said. "Almost there."

She grabbed her backpack and rushed to join Bernard in the cockpit.

Jordan turned his attention back to Eldon. "I want to ask you something. Don't think I'm crazy, but do you ever wonder if Chupacabra's right? About my grandfather."

Eldon looked at Jordan very seriously, and Jordan continued. "What I mean is, do you ever wonder why Chupacabra's so sure my Grampa Grimsley's still alive?"

Eldon sat back and thought about this. "Chupacabra's twisted with hatred and vengeance. He's been obsessed with getting back at George Grimsley for so long, he's convinced himself that George Grimsley is still out there."

"But—" Jordan glanced toward the cockpit, where Abbie was talking with Bernard. He suddenly spoke in a lower voice. "That's the thing. I don't know what it is . . . but I think I'm beginning to feel it, too."

"You're not crazy. But you do have something in common with Chupacabra. You both want to believe George Grimsley's alive. For very different reasons, of course, but just as strongly." Eldon reached down and picked up Grampa Grimsley's old journal off the floor where it had fallen from Jordan's arms during the long overnight flight. He flipped through pages filled with George Grimsley's sketches of cryptids, drawings of maps of faraway places, and handwritten entries describing his adventures and discoveries. Near the end of the journal, Eldon noticed different handwriting. He looked up at Jordan, who shrugged.

"I'm adding some of what I've learned. I figured it wouldn't matter to anyone."

Eldon smiled and handed the journal back. "It matters a lot. You're continuing the Grimsley legacy. Your grandfather *is* still alive, Jordan. Through you."

As he took the journal back, something caught Jordan's eye. Eldon's finger. On it was his Grampa Grimsley's crystal ring. He could see the sparkling liquid inside of it—a very special concentrated elixir of the Fountain of Youth. It seemed to dance and swirl inside the thick, clear band. Eldon noticed.

"It's still yours, y'know. Whenever you're ready to claim it. Your grandfather passed it along to me to lead the Creature Keepers, but you're its rightful owner."

Bernard poked his head out of the cockpit. "We're within five miles of the signal. Switching engines to chopper mode to get over a safe drop zone." They looked up. Abbie was standing over them, holding a pair of parachutes. She was grinning.

"Drop zone?" Jordan said, now on his feet. "We're not landing?"

"Oh, you're landing," Abbie said, handing Eldon a parachute. She tossed the other one at her brother. "And I hope it's a soft one for you guys."

Jordan and Eldon traded glances as they put on their parachutes. Bernard stepped out of the cockpit and pulled open the sliding door. The wind whipped into the Heli-Jet cabin, and they could see the vast desert below. Jordan was terrified. And confused.

"Wait, I didn't know we were skydiving in." Jordan glanced at Eldon. "Did you?" Eldon shrugged and stepped toward the open door. Jordan looked back at his grinning sister. "What about you? Aren't you coming?"

"Nah, you got this," Abbie said. "Go take care of the turd situation. Bernard and I are going to pop over to Japan and check on Katsu and Shika's creature."

"What?" Jordan hollered over the whipping wind from the open door.

Abbie grinned back at him. "I promised Shika. This should save us some time."

"Wait!" Jordan saw Eldon clearly trying to hide a smile. He turned back to his sister. "This wasn't the plan! *Jumping out of this plane was not the plan!*"

"Plan's changed," Abbie said, shoving the T-549 at him. "We'll swing back to pick you up. Right after you scoop that poop!" Abbie stepped toward her brother and shoved him out the door. Then she turned to Eldon.

"Pretty impressive, Elite Keeper." He gave her a smile, then turned and jumped out of the Heli-Jet.

Abbie slid the door closed and locked it. Bernard was standing in the cockpit door, his mouth hanging open.

"What are you staring at?" she said. "Fire up those thrusters! Next stop, Japan."

It was afternoon by the time Abbie and Bernard had crossed the Sea of Japan. Bernard flew low to the water as they approached the northern part of the country, staying close to the green treetops. Finally, he lowered the airship, touching down in a clearing deep within the Shirakami-Sanchi Forest. The two of them slid open the door and looked out at the thick, bushy beech trees and the nearby Anmon River winding its way through them.

Abbie had been reading the *Raising and Caring for Your Kappa* book that Shika had given her. "It says here that most of this forest is protected and isolated. But just in case, you'd better stay with the jet and keep out of sight."

Bernard slumped a little. "Okay," he said, disappointed. He nodded toward a grove. "I picked up Morris on the onboard GCPS. Follow the river into that grove. He's in there somewhere. You sure you should be doing this?"

"I have to. I made a promise to a girl who, despite calling me her BFF, still deserves to know that her creature is okay. Failure is not an option." She hopped out of the Heli-Jet onto the soft forest floor, then turned and smiled at Bernard. "Also, it'll really annoy my brother."

The low-lying beech-tree branches, with their feather-like leaves, gave the forest a dreamlike quality. As she made her way along the banks of the Anmon River, Abbie glanced up at the wispy green giants bending and arching over her head. The afternoon sunlight splintered through their leaves, casting a peaceful glow. The water splashed and tumbled, snaking its way through the trees, leading Abbie deeper into the forest.

"Morris!" she called out over the whispering forest. "Morris, if you can hear me, I'm a friend of Shika's! It's okay for you to show yourself!"

A strange cry answered her calls, stopping her in her tracks and sending a chill down her back. It came from just across the river, from inside a thick collection of trunks. It was a sort of guttural crowing, like a chicken with a head cold. She crossed the river, stepping on mossy stones, and reached the other side.

"Morris?"

"*Errhhh!*" The strange sound called out louder this time, from behind a cluster of trees just ahead of her. She ran to it and immediately felt her legs yank out from under her. A second later, she was trapped, hanging upside down by her ankles over the forest floor, suspended by a rope that had been pulleyed through the branches overhead.

She wanted to scream, but stopped herself when she was faced with her captor. He was a human boy with Asian features. And he looked just as frightened as she was.

"Who are you?" Abbie yelled at him. "Let me down right now!"

"Who are *you*? This forest is protected. You are not supposed to be here!"

"Neither are you," Abbie said. The two of them eyed each other suspiciously, neither wanting to be the first to speak.

"You were yelling for the Kappa!" the boy finally blurted out.

"Well, you were making weird Kappa noises! Ha! Busted!"

"How do you know what Morris sounds like? Aha! Busted back!"

Abbie reached behind her and yanked open her backpack. The contents tumbled out onto the ground, including *Raising and Caring for Your Kappa*. The boy picked it up and looked at it. "Where did you get this?"

"From Shika. Not that it's any of your business."

"You don't know Shika. *I* know Shika."

"Excuse me, but she and I are besties." Abbie couldn't believe the words that just came out of her mouth. She hoped it was the blood rushing to her head. "I'm here on an official Creature Keeper mission, if that means anything to you."

"I know all about the Creature Keepers. But how do I know *you* know about the Creature Keepers?"

There was a snapping sound behind them. Abbie suddenly dropped to the ground. The skinny boy spun around. Bernard stood holding the cut rope.

"I can vouch for her," he said calmly. "Also, she has a shiny badge."

Abbie stood up and shoved her Elite Keeper badge in the boy's face.

A moment later, Zaya was leading Abbie and Bernard along the riverside, deeper into the beech-tree forest, until they finally came to a small clearing beside the river.

There in front of them was a large, stone statue of a creature. It had a turtle-like shell for a back, thick scaly-carved legs, and an oversized head.

"Okay," Abbie said. "Nice statue. Now where is the *actual* Kappa?"

"This is him!" Zaya said. "This is how I found him!"

Abbie and Bernard exchanged a worried look. She stepped to the statue and touched it. It was solid rock. She looked it over closely, studying its features. They perfectly matched the description and pictures in her book. Its face had two large, lazy eyes and a beak-like nose. And its head was deeply concave at the top, like a soup bowl. Its webbed claws were raised, as if trying to reach into the bowl, or protect it. That's when Abbie noticed something. The only thing on the entire statue not made of stone was around the statue's wrist. One of Jordan's GCPS tracker bracelets. She removed it and showed it to Bernard. "He's telling the truth. I think this is Morris."

"Can you help him?" Zaya said.

"For a river cryptid, he's pretty far from the river," Bernard said.

Abbie was scanning the *Raising and Caring for Your Kappa* book. A terrible feeling had come over her as she imagined telling Shika how they found her creature. "Here," she said, consulting the book. "The deep indentation in his head is called a *sara*. It needs to stay filled with water. It says here that if it empties . . . he turns to stone."

"Is it permanent?" Bernard asked sadly.

"That depends." Abbie's nose was in the book. "Within each monthly cycle of the moon, he can refill and come back to life only two times. If he spills a third time before this phase of the moon rises again, he stays stone forever." She held up a page of the book and showed them a picture of a half-lit moon. It was shaped like a turtle's shell.

"That's the First Quarter phase," Bernard said.

47

"It comes every four weeks. And if I'm not mistaken, the next one rises in seven days." Abbie and Zaya both looked at him. "I'm a bit of an astronomy buff." Bernard shrugged.

"So, depending on how many times he's spilled this month, we might be able to bring him back to life by refilling his sara," Zaya said.

"What are we waiting for?" Abbie suddenly exclaimed.

Bernard and Zaya leaped into action, pushing hard against the stone turtle cryptid, trying to move him toward the nearby river. Bernard was a very strong creature, and not just in odor. He was quite muscular under his smelly fur. And yet he couldn't budge the immobilized cryptid. "This thing is a lot heavier than it looks," he said between grunts.

As the two of them continued with all their might, Abbie set down her book, walked to the edge of the babbling Anmon River, bent down, and scooped the cool water with her hands. She carried it back, then gently released it into the empty bowl atop Morris's head. Bernard and Zaya noticed, stopped pushing, and stepped back.

A glossy dampness spread down through Morris's stone face, as if he'd sprung a leak from the inside.

It steadily transformed the dry, brown solid rock to moist, bluish-green scales, claws, and shell. His large, heavy-lidded eyes blinked and looked around. Then they fell directly on Abbie.

"Hello, master," the Kappa said to her in a soft, croaking voice. His rounded beak smacked dryly. "I seem to be parched. Might I trouble you for a drink of water?"

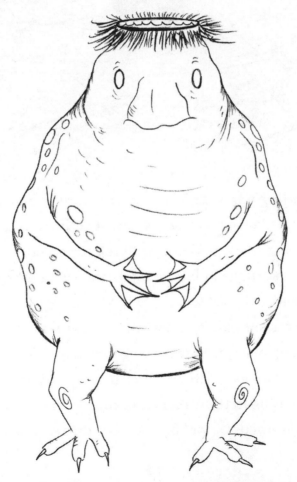

A howling wind slammed against Jordan and Eldon as they made their way across a vast desert of Xinjiang. The two of them had been walking for an hour across a bare and rugged plain, the gusts slowing every step they took.

"Just keep moving forward!" Eldon shouted back. "And keep one eye on that tracker gizmo of yours!"

Jordan's mobile GCPS tracker device was presumably pointing in the direction of the collar Chupacabra had swallowed. Unfortunately, that direction was also

leading them head-on into an approaching sandstorm that barreled toward them across the flat, barren land.

As the wind and sand picked up, they huddled together tightly and braced themselves. The sand blotted out the sun overhead and nearly buried the two of them as it passed. Then, suddenly, a quiet calm settled over the desert. Jordan blew the sand off his device and stared down at it. "C'mon," he hollered. "Let's keep going while we can!"

Eldon got up and knocked the sand out of his ears.

"I have to say, I wasn't too keen on that newfangled system you and Doris installed. But even if I don't completely understand it, I'm glad we have it in place. Especially now."

"Between those wandering cryptids and whatever we find out here in the desert, this gizmo of mine will be the key to us figuring out what's going on," Jordan said, staring down at his device as he walked. "You'll be thanking me! I still don't get why you're so against technology, anyway."

"It's a load of dung!"

Jordan looked up, irritated. "Hey! That's not very nice."

Eldon was peering through his beat-up-looking binoculars as he pointed. "No! Up ahead! I think I see a load of dung!"

In the distance was a small brown blob, the only other object besides themselves for miles and miles. Jordan and Eldon ran toward it. Soon they were standing over what looked to be a greenish-brown pile. Eldon immediately dropped to his belly and began sniffing it. Jordan made a face.

"Ew. Chupa-poop. So that's bad, right?"

Eldon took another good whiff, then put on a pair of rubber gloves and gently poked the dropping. Jordan could tell Eldon was utilizing his skills in spooring—an ancient tracking technique very popular with Badger Rangers. After his inspection, Eldon offered his analysis. "The sample is surprisingly moist for its environment, which would indicate a freshness. And yet it lacks the pungent odor of a recent deposit."

"Well, pungent or moist or whatever, it's most definitely our dropping. Look." Tightly bound to the poop was Syd's beat-up, half-digested, weather-worn GCPS tracking device. "That's our tracker, which means Chupacabra could be alive."

"And he could be anywhere," Eldon added. He stood and wandered a few feet away, carefully spooring the sand for tracks. "Strange. As fresh as that sample is, I see no evidence whatsoever of Chupacabra."

Jordan pulled out the T-549 pooper-scooper and put on his rubber gloves. "In these conditions, any tracks would've been blown away."

"Yes," Eldon said. "So why didn't it blow away the scat, as well?"

Jordan thought about this, then turned his attention to the scat at hand. He knelt down and looked closer at his GCPS collar tightly wound around the pile. He noticed a small transmitter box attached to the collar. Printed on it were five letters: CHUPA. "That is not part of my design," he said to himself. Jordan pulled at the collar, but it didn't budge. He pulled out his pocket-knife, opened the blade and jabbed at the turd with the tip.

RUMMMBBBLLLE! A mild tremor suddenly shook the ground all around them. Jordan dropped his knife and looked up at Eldon, who was still spooring for nearby tracks. "Earthquake?" Jordan said.

"Not normal for this region."

Jordan swallowed hard. A cold fear grew in his stomach as he imagined something awful. "Soil-Soles?" The two of them stared across the desert plain in every direction, searching for a sign of Chupacabra armed—or rather footed—with one of the Sasquatch's earth-rumbling Soil-Soles. Thankfully, there didn't seem to be a single other living thing for what appeared to be hundreds of miles.

"I don't think so," Eldon said. "There's no one out here but us."

Jordan turned his attention back to the pile. He took the knife and poked the turd again, but harder this time.

ZAPOW! A flash of blue-white lightning suddenly sent Jordan flying into the air, knocking him back. Jordan shook the sand out of his hair and tried to sit up as

Eldon ran toward him, his miniature first-aid kit out of his backpack and at the ready.

"Did you see that?" Jordan asked.

"Don't move," Eldon answered. "You were nearly struck by lightning, and could be in shock."

"That's the thing—I think the lightning shot out of that turd!"

"Okay, you need to just rest for a minute." He held Jordan's wrist and checked his pulse. "You're clearly dazed, and a little confused."

Jordan looked past Eldon's concerned expression

at the scat lying on the desert floor. He'd seen a lot of weird things since he'd met the Creature Keepers. A lightning-charged pile of poo didn't seem out of the question.

Abbie watched as Morris dropped yet another slimy fish on the pile at her feet. "Thanks again, Morris. But you can stop bringing me fish now. I need you to listen to me."

"As you wish, master." Morris began to bow to her. As he did a splash of water sloshed over the top of his head.

"Morris, no! What are you doing?"

"It is my tradition to bow to my new master, master."

"Okay, couple of things. If you bow, you spill. And if you spill again before the next Quarter Moon rises—you could, uh. It would just be bad. So no bowing, got it?"

"As you wish, master."

"Which brings me to my second thing. I'm not your master. I'm a friend of Katsu and Shika. Your *Keepers*. They asked me to come check on you, that's all. Got it?"

"You replenished my sara," Morris said. "You are my master now."

"No, Morris. I mean, yes, I did that, but Katsu and Shika, they're—"

"They emptied my sara. You filled it. You are my master now."

Abbie stared into his large, glassy eyes. Zaya, who had been pacing near the river, looked over at him.

Abbie thought for a moment as Bernard walked up, bent down, and effortlessly lifted Morris straight up over his head, careful not to spill his head-bowl. "Just checking," he said, setting the Kappa back down. "Wanted to make sure I hadn't lost my brute strength. That water diet we put you on has really helped you shed the pounds, Morris. Like, a thousand of them."

He headed off into the forest. "I'm going to go back and get the Heli-Jet ready for takeoff. We need to pick up the other two before nightfall."

Zaya rushed over to them. "Morris, did you say it was your Keepers who emptied your sara?"

Morris looked down. "I don't really like thinking about it," he said sadly.

•

"I remember back at the CKCC," Abbie said. "Eldon mentioned something about Morris being left in a state where no one could harm him. Turning him to solid stone must be what he meant. It was the safest way to protect him, I suppose."

"No!" Zaya was suddenly upset. "Why would my Corky be the only one?"

Abbie turned to him. "What are you talking about? Who's Corky?"

"My cryptid. She was hypnotized by some mutant creature, put into a sleep state. I tried to wake her, but I couldn't. I couldn't help her."

"Wait. Mutant creature? What mutant creature?"

"Freakish-looking beast. Strange green reptilian scales, but a doglike face. And one giant foot. Like he was built from different parts."

"Chupacabra," Abbie said.

"He paralyzed my Corky, but spared me. Let me go so I could tell others what had happened. He said he'd do the same to all cryptids who didn't join him. I didn't know where to go, so I came to warn my neighbors, Katsu and Shika, and make sure they were safe. But when I arrived, they were gone, and their creature was paralyzed, too."

"And you thought this mutant creature did to Morris what he did to Corky?"

Zaya nodded sadly. "It's why I booby-trapped the forest. In case that thing came back. And then you showed up. I was hoping that if an Elite Keeper came all this way to save Morris, you might save Corky next." He looked at Abbie with eyes full of tears. "Can you? Can you help me?"

"Of course," Abbie said. "But if we're dealing with who it sounds like, we'll definitely need to go to the Xinjiang Desert first, to get my brother and Eldon."

"The Xinjiang Desert? That's where Corky is!"

Abbie's mind was suddenly reeling. "I thought you said you were neighbors!"

"Out here 'neighbors' is a relative term. It's not like in the West, where you couldn't swing a Mongolian Death Worm without hitting another cryptid."

Abbie stared at him for a moment. A chill ran down her spine. "Zaya. What and where, exactly, is your creature from?"

"Corky's the Mongolian Death Worm," he said.

"From Mongolia?"

"Oh, no."

"We lived happily beneath the great Gobi Desert in southern Mongolia until that horrible mutant showed up. It brainwashed Corky. Before I knew what was happening, Corky had burrowed southward beneath the sand, tunneling away from our home. Away from me. I followed them for hundreds of miles, all the way to the middle of nowhere."

"The Xinjiang Desert. Oh, no, no, no . . ."

"That's where I found her, fast asleep underground, just her tail sticking out of the desert floor, unable to wake up." Zaya sniffled as he pulled out a crumpled photo. "Here's a picture of the two of us together, in happier times."

"Oh, no, no, no, no, *no*!" she said, gazing at the picture. "We have to go. We have to go *right now*!"

Abbie and Zaya raced back toward the Heli-Jet, running as fast as they could along the bank of the Anmon River. Swimming alongside them, Morris happily zipped through the water like a torpedo.

Bernard stood in the open Heli-Jet cargo door with a look of concern on his furry face. Abbie yelled to him as they approached.

"Start the engine!" she cried out. "We have to get back to the desert right away! I think the whole thing might be a trap set by Chupacabra!"

Bernard turned to do as he was ordered, but stopped and pointed past them. "What about him?"

Abbie and Zaya turned around. Morris stood at the edge of the Anmon River, almost as frozen as when he was made of stone. He looked up at them, then back down at the water rushing past his webbed feet.

"Morris, c'mon!" Abbie yelled to him. "We have to go!"

Morris went to take a step out of the river, then stopped.

"What's wrong with him?" Zaya said.

"Morris," Abbie called out. "We don't have time for games. I need you to come with us now!"

"As you wish, master," Morris said with a tremble in his voice. He lifted his foot, then raised his arms to his bowl-head, checking that it was still full of river water. He lowered his leg and looked up at her.

Abbie suddenly realized something. "Morris, is that what happened with your Keepers? Did they ask you to come out of the river before they—?" Morris nodded slightly, his water bowl sloshing around. Abbie reached up and put a hand on each of his scaly cheeks. "Listen to me," she said carefully. "I wouldn't do that. You can trust me. I won't let anything happen to you. Do you understand?"

Morris smiled a little, then struggled to lift his leg out of the water. "I'm trying, master. I know I need to do what you say, I just—"

"No, Morris. You don't have to do what I say. You have to think for yourself. It's up to you. But I have an emergency. People I care about, as well as another cryptid like you, may be in very real danger. I don't want to risk leaving you here alone, but I can't make you come. It's your decision. But I'm afraid you have to decide right now."

Morris looked at her, then glanced down at his river home. She held out her hand. He slowly raised his claw. It was trembling.

"Hold on!" Bernard bounded toward them with something in his hand. He bent down at the edge of the river. When he turned around, he had a big grin on his face. In his hand was his plastic "THIRST AID" drinking helmet. Two apple juice boxes on either side were filled with river water, and the straws that had siphoned apple juice into the Skunk Ape's mouth earlier were redirected to flow back into the air holes at the top of the helmet. Bernard stepped toward Morris and held it out to him.

"Ta-da!" he said. "Hands-free beverage helmet and automatic sara replenisher!"

"Bernard, you're a genius," Abbie said.

The helmet fit snugly over the lip of Morris's concave sara, tightly covering the bowl, sealing the water inside. The reserve tanks were at the ready, able to top off any water that might seep out. Morris smiled more confidently. He took a deep breath and stepped out of the river, onto dry land. "Thank you," he said, tapping a clawed finger to his new helmet. "It's a lovely hat. You're sure you don't mind?"

A moment later, Zaya strapped Morris into a flight seat on the Heli-Jet as Abbie joined Bernard in the cockpit. "Okay. How fast can you get us back to Xinjiang?"

"This baby can move pretty fast," he said. "What's going on?"

"I hope I'm wrong, but I think Chupacabra may have set a trap to try to hook himself a Creature Keeper or two. And for bait he's using a really, really big worm."

"I'm okay! Knock it off!" Jordan sat on the ground as Eldon continued to attack him with a tongue depressor, miniature stethoscope, and disposable blood-pressure gauge. He'd pulled out nearly everything in his official Badger Ranger first-aid kit, and was prodding and poking at Jordan like he was an overcooked chicken.

"You were nearly struck by lightning," Eldon said as he packed up his kit and returned his attention to the sand surrounding the dung pile. "You're lucky to be alive."

Jordan cautiously approached the little pile of dung. He figured Eldon was right—he must've been in a state of shock when he imagined a lightning bolt had burst out of it. Deciding that he wasn't going to

let a little sunbaked cryptid dropping get the best of him, he picked up the pooper-scooper and swung the metal spade back. Then, with all the force he had, he slammed it into the base of the pile.

RUUUMMMBLLLE! The ground erupted in a trembling quake. The sand beneath Jordan's feet shifted, then dropped, as if sifting into a sinkhole. Jordan's feet were caught up in it, and he stumbled backward, as— *ZAPOW!*—a burst of lightning shot into the sky. There was no doubt this time—it came directly out of the tip of that dung heap.

"JORDAN!"

He saw Eldon rush toward him, then stop at the edge of the sinkhole that was swirling around both Jordan and the pile of dung—*which was now moving.* The turd wriggled and squirmed, shifting and stirring the sand, as it sank deeper.

ZAPOW! Another lightning blast shot out of the

dung tip. Jordan tried to dive away from it, but his feet were buried. Then his ankles. Then his knees.

"Jordan! That's not scat! Quick! Grab hold of the T-549!"

Eldon waved the pooper-scooper over Jordan's head. He reached for it but slipped deeper, following the false turd as it wriggled violently into the swirling sand. Jordan looked down and spotted something terrifying. That little lightning-charged non-turd seemed to be, in fact, the tail end of a very large creature. And that creature was working its way straight down, caving in the ground beneath Jordan along with it.

Glancing back up, the last thing Jordan saw before being sucked underground was Eldon's face looking over the edge of the sinkhole. The two boys made eye contact for a second, and then Jordan was engulfed in total darkness.

Churning sand flew past Jordan's face as he fell downward. He reached out for the deadly tail tip and pulled himself onto the back of the creature. He knew if he didn't catch a ride and get pulled through by whatever this horrible thing was, he might be left behind and buried alive. Holding on to its slimy back was like trying to hug a giant, overfilled water balloon. As it tunneled, Jordan slid toward the tail of the creature.

His foot snagged on something like a strap. Even in the dark, Jordan knew what this was. He kept his foot tucked in the tracker collar attached to the creature's tail as if it were a stirrup on a horse. The creature leveled off, tunneling horizontally deep beneath the ground. Jordan saw that it was leaving a clean tunnel in its wake, and he thought for a second of letting go and backtracking out to Eldon. That notion was quickly ruled out, however, as a crack of lightning burst from the tip of the creature's tail, blasting white light down the tunnel behind it. Jordan decided to shut his eyes and hold on tight.

The wild, dark ride suddenly ended in a large, dimly lit underground chamber. As the creature slid to a stop, it flicked its tail, sending Jordan flying. *WHAM!* He slammed into a far dirt wall and slid down onto the cold ground. His eyes adjusted to the light and he noticed candles glowing throughout the cavern. He also could make out in the shadows the beast that had transported him to this strange place. It squirmed toward the opposite side of the cavern, then coiled up in the corner. It was a gigantic, hideous worm creature, at least fifty feet long, with four tiny, beady black eyes indented in its veiny head. Limbless, its fleshy body was ribbed like that of an earthworm, all the way down to the end of its turd-like tail. There, tightly choking the very tip, was Syd's old GCPS tracking bracelet—the one that had been swallowed by Chupacabra.

The opposite end of the worm suddenly rose up. It opened its gaping mouth to reveal long, curving teeth, each one the size and shape of a pickax. It hissed at Jordan, and a spray of hot saliva shot out of some gland deep in the back of its throat.

A bodiless voice echoed within the chamber, startling Jordan. "Now, now, Corky. Where are your manners? George Grimsley is our guest. Please. Try not to spit on him."

The worm immediately recoiled, as did Jordan. This was a voice he knew all too well. And even if he didn't recognize it, there was only one person—or in this case one cryptid—who would call him by the name of his grandfather. It was Chupacabra.

Peering into the dim light, Jordan could make out a shadowy figure petting the worm's fleshy head. "Here, have a snack, Corky, it'll help you to relax," the shadow said. He tossed something into Corky's gaping mouth. The air suddenly took on an odor of smelly feet.

As Chupacabra stepped slowly toward Jordan, he seemed to avoid the patches of candlelight, staying in the darkness. Behind the approaching shadow, the worm's giant head began to bob and nod as it grew drowsy, until it lowered onto the ground and passed out. From what Jordan could make out in the candle-light, there was only one way out—the tunnel he'd come in through. And that was being blocked by a gigantic worm's coiled, unconscious body.

The shadow's red eyes glowed in the darkness. "He loves those snacks," Chupacabra's voice echoed. "My own special recipe, made from a very rare Siberian valerian root. I've found it causes a sort of sleepwalking state in not only the Mongolian Death Worm, but nearly all cryptids. I discovered the plant on a recent trip. Oh, but what am I saying—you were there! Remember the lovely send-off you gave me?"

"Yes," Jordan said, his voice trembling. "And it should have killed you." The dark figure stood in the shadows, directly before him.

"Well, I must say that thanks to you I feel quite reborn. That jet thruster blasted me back to my true self, with no disguises and no one to help me. It forced me back to my old ways—creeping through the night, lying low by day, avoiding being hunted, simply surviving! It's how I lived when you first exposed me to the world, all those years ago. You remember, don't you, Georgie?"

"For the last time, that was my grandfather. Not me," Jordan said. "And I'm sorry he did that to you. But he's gone now. You need to stop being a jerk and hurting people."

"DON'T LIE TO ME!" Chupacabra's face pitched forward, catching the candlelight, giving Jordan his first glimpse at the creature since he'd scorched him with the jet thruster. Jordan could feel his hot breath. "I never forget the scent of an enemy, Georgie boy. Yours may be faint beneath your elixirs and disguises, but I can still smell you in this chamber."

Chupacabra stood up straight again, plunging his face back into the darkness. "That blast didn't just destroy my power to change into human form—as it burned away the pathetic mask of Señor Areck Gusto, it welded into place the creature I was always meant to be . . . with a few minor improvements, of course."

Chupacabra finally stepped into the light. Jordan couldn't believe his eyes. He knew Chupacabra had taken the Loch Ness Monster's Hydro-Hide and turned it into a coat of her powerful scales. And he was all too aware that Chupacabra had gotten away with one of the Sasquatch's Soil-Soles. Jordan had seen these "improvements" the last time he faced Chupacabra. They looked silly and mismatched on him then. But this was different. Something had changed. And not for the better.

Chupacabra's suit of scales from Nessie's Hydro-Hide was now seared to his body, like it had become part of him. They had a green, glazed glimmer that Jordan didn't recognize. Syd's Soil-Sole on Chupacabra's left foot was still oversized compared to his right, but it too had melded to his body in a more natural-looking way. In a word, Chupacabra now looked—

"Rather impressive, wouldn't you say?" The cryptid grinned. "Not only were you instrumental in helping me acquire these little gifts, but by blasting me with fire, you also fused my newfound elements into one, making me something of a . . . *super-cryptid*."

"You have no right to those powers," Jordan said. "They're not yours to keep."

"Says who? You? That's the problem with you and your Creature Keeping organization, George. So many rules! Of course, with all your well-thought-out guide-lines on how to 'protect' my kind, you forgot one very important thing—rules are for men, not creatures. We're not meant to abide by your plan to have us live in the shadows. Far from it! Throughout history, we cryptids sprang from the earth's most explosive and destructive moments. And our history will be your downfall. But you won't recognize when history repeats itself, Georgie, even as it's happening all around you. Because you never bothered to learn it in the first place. By the time Operation Pangaea has begun, there won't be anything you can do about it. Even your prized three special creatures won't be able to stop me."

"I don't know what you're talking about."

"My point exactly." He fluttered his Hydro-Hide scales and wiggled the bulbous toes of his single Soil-Sole, admiring his appearance. "Yes, you discovered and successfully brainwashed those three special cryptids. The ones endowed with elemental powers, they think they're so superior. But did you ever try to find out where they came from, or even wonder why they had such unique gifts? That Scottish sea cow you all worship was bestowed a Hydro-Hide to control the seas and oceans. And that idiotic ape you call Bigfoot? He was foolishly given the dangerous element of his Soil-Soles to command earth and stone. But we all evolve, Georgie. And now, thanks to you, evolution has passed their sacred gifts along to me."

"You mean you stole them. You're not special like them. You're just a two-bit thief."

"That's an amazing bit of name-calling coming

from you, Georgie boy. You who created your little group to steal my kind from the world, stashing us out of sight, stuffing us into caves, brainwashing us to believe we actually needed your protection! Even after all this time, you still don't really know what you're dealing with. I feel sorry for you."

Chupacabra leaned in closer. "Tell you what. Since you're about to help me once again, I'll enlighten you with a little secret. There aren't *three* elemental powers in the cryptid world, as your sad little squad has always believed. There are *four*! And as with the first two, you will be the one who helps me complete my collection. Once I possess all four elemental powers, nothing will stop me. And that will be the end of your world as you know it, sealing the fate of your kind to history, forever."

"Whatever powers you steal, the Creature Keepers will stop you!"

Chupacabra stood up straight and tall. "Well, you certainly have tried. And as you said yourself, Georgie, I should already be dead." He spun around, showing off his upgrades again. "But it seems whatever you try that doesn't kill me . . . only makes me stronger! *Ha-ha-ha-ha!*"

Chupacabra's horrible laugh echoed throughout

the chamber as he fluttered his Hydro-Hide. The scales flashed in the candlelight, shooting dots of light throughout the cavern. He lifted his Soil-Sole and stomped it on the ground. The entire cavern trembled, and great chunks of sand and dirt fell down all around Jordan.

The Heli-Jet zoomed westward across the Sea of Japan, toward the great desert plains of northwest China. Abbie stood beside Bernard, who glanced down at the built-in GCPS navigation system Jordan had installed in the cockpit. "Our mystery tracker bracelet has moved across the desert," he said. "Not far, but it moved."

"Head for it," Abbie said. "Wherever that tracker is, that's where we'll find them. I just hope we're not too late. Any word from Creature Keeper central command?"

"Still trying to get through to them. It's important that we don't panic."

"Good advice. Thanks, Bernard." She turned to

check on Morris and bumped into Zaya, who was standing right behind her in the cockpit doorway. "Sorry," he said. "Anything I can do to help?"

Abbie shook her head. "Not 'til we get there and see what we're dealing with."

Zaya fidgeted. "Corky's not a bad worm. I know she can seem intimidating, with her dagger-sharp teeth. And the glands in the back of her throat that spray hot spit mixed with whatever she ate last. Oh, and she does tend to shoot lightning out of her tail when she's startled or awoken suddenly." Zaya thought for a second. "Okay, when I say all that out loud, she sounds horrible. And dangerous. Especially on each of her ends. But trust me—her middle section is all squishy and warm. It's really quite nice."

"She sounds like a real snuggle-muffin," Abbie said. "Look, whatever Corky's up to, I'm sure it's because Chupacabra's controlling her. As far as I'm concerned, this mission is to rescue three members of the Creature Keeper family: super-dork Eldon, my wimpy brother, Jordan, and that wonderful little pet of yours. Okay?"

Zaya smiled. "Okay."

Off to the side, Morris was buckled up in one of the passenger seats, wearing his sippy-helmet and gazing out the window.

Abbie sat down next to him. "Morris, how are you doing?"

"I should be asking you that, master," Morris said with a gentle smile.

"Listen, I'm happy to help you, because that's my job—as a Creature Keeper."

"*Elite* Creature Keeper," Morris said. "Do not undersell yourself, master."

Abbie smiled. "But here's the thing. You've gotta learn to think and be responsible for yourself. You're your own master. Think about this. Okay?"

"As you wish!" Morris shut his eyes tightly. It looked like he was in a deep state of concentration. Abbie rolled her eyes, then stood up.

"Of all the cryptids I could have gotten as a devoted slave, I get a turtle-child who can't spill his water bowl."

Bernard spoke from the cockpit. "I got the CKCC. Doris is on!"

Abbie jumped in the copilot's seat and grabbed the transmitter. "Doris! You there? Hello?"

The radio crackled a bit, then Doris's voice burst through the static. "Denmother Doris here! I read you loud and clear. How are you all doing?"

"We're fine. Heading back to find Eldon and Jordan now. Please tell Shika and Katsu that Morris is with us, and all's fine and normal. Y'know, relatively speaking."

"Roger that, dearie. Listen, there's been some movement on that tracker device you're going after. It moved south about ten miles or so, then stopped again."

"We know. We're following it. We'll report in as soon as we can."

"All right, but there's something else. We're seeing even more tracking devices belonging to cryptids farther south of you wandering off again—places like Madagascar, Sri Lanka, Indonesia. Mac and Nessie are on damage control, but they've got their hands—and fins—full. There's also another weird thing—the wandering cryptids all seem to be headed in the same direction, toward the collar device you're tracking. Got any clue as to what in tarnation is going on?"

"Not yet, Doris. But we're on our way to pick up the two dorks who might. We'll let you know as soon as we find out. Over and out." Abbie hung up the transmitter and shared a nervous glance with Bernard.

"You can panic a little now, if you want," Bernard said.

"Just keep following that signal," Abbie said. "And find those two dorks."

"If you think I'm going to help you, then you're even crazier than you look." Jordan was still backed against the wall, watching Chupacabra as he mashed up a grayish-green root with a stone mortar and pestle. It gave off a horrible, stinky-foot smell. Behind him, Corky the Mongolian Death Worm was still in a deep sleep.

"Aw, don't talk like that, Georgie," Chupacabra said. "It hurts my feelings. Besides, you owe me this one."

"Now you're really making no sense," Jordan said. "I owe you nothing."

"Your recklessness made me more powerful, but you and the rest of your Creature Keepers still managed

to derail my master plan not once but twice. First by saving the life of that overgrown guppy, allowing her to grow back her Hydro-Hide, and then by letting the Sasquatch steal back one of his Soil-Soles! Do you have any idea how annoying that was? With either of those elements exclusively in my possession, I could have pulled off my plan without the need for the next elemental power. But you ruined that, so you will now lead me to the next one. After all, you're the only one who knows where it is, Georgie. Which is the only reason you're still alive."

"Well, you make a good argument. There's just one problem: *I'M NOT GEORGE GRIMSLEY!*"

Chupacabra sniffed the air again. "The nose knows, Georgie boy. The nose knows."

As the cryptid continued mashing the smelly root, something at the other end of the chamber caught Jordan's attention. He wasn't sure if it was the shadows playing tricks on his eyes, but there seemed to be something moving near the tunnel entrance. As it disappeared behind Corky, Jordan glanced back at Chupacabra.

"And should you refuse to help me," the cryptid casually continued, "or if that feeble old brain of yours has forgotten where I can find it, I'll just have to drag you along with me on my search until your memory kicks in. High altitudes can really clear the mind. And it doesn't get any higher than in the Himalayas. We'll start at the top of the world and work our way on down, one mountaintop at a time. Eventually you'll lead me to what I need, and one step closer to controlling the power of the Perfect Storm."

Jordan pretended to listen to Chupacabra as he scanned the shadowy cave behind him. He could make out Corky's body gently heaving up and down in a deep sleep, and as she exhaled, he spotted it—the tippy-top of a very distinctive hat. A First-Class Badger Ranger hat. Jordan tried to remain expressionless, even as he saw Eldon move to the face of the sleeping beast. Eldon had his first-aid kit out and was using tongue depressors to lift the creature's rubbery eyelids so he could stare into its black eyeballs. *I don't believe this*, Jordan thought. *Eldon is giving a sleeping Mongolian Death Worm a physical examination.*

"Do you have nothing to say?" Chupacabra was suddenly glaring at Jordan.

"I . . . erm . . . I guess I'm just dumbfounded by your impressive masterminding," Jordan said. "It's kind of stunning, to be perfectly honest with you."

"You're lying, but not wrong. And you don't even know the half of it. Once I have the power of the Perfect Storm, nothing will stop me from carrying out my final plan."

"Yes, yes. Operation Pangaea, right? Please, tell me more about this awesome plan?" Jordan asked. He needed to keep Chupacabra distracted from whatever Eldon was up to, and talking about himself was one thing Jordan noticed the evil cryptid couldn't resist.

"It's simple, Georgie." Chupacabra chuckled. "I just want to bring the world closer together, that's all."

As he continued to snicker at his evil genius, Jordan

glanced back at Corky. Eldon had apparently completed his exam and had moved back to the tail. He was pushing against it as quietly as he could, gradually repositioning the rear tip of the Death Worm until it pointed directly at the back of Chupacabra. He caught Jordan's eye and gestured for him to duck out of the way.

ssssHHH!

"Oh, no," Jordan said.

"Oh, yes!" Chupacabra replied. "And it will usher

in a cataclysmic event that will give birth to one all-powerful cryptid to rule over the entire planet! *HAHAHA!*"

As Chupacabra threw his head back in laughter, Eldon's head popped up again near Corky's face. He opened his kit and pulled out what appeared to be a small twig. He glanced at Jordan, then at Corky's tail. Then he held up three fingers. Then two. Then he snapped the stick in half, right under one of Corky's nostrils.

The worm's eyes popped open. So did Chupacabra's. Whatever the small twig was, breaking it had given off an immediate and pungent odor. Chupacabra spun around as Jordan leaped out of the way. Waking up so suddenly from the natural smelling salts, the giant worm sprayed the cave with her glandular sand-spit.

Then her tail went off—the same tail that Eldon had aimed directly at Chupacabra.

ZAPOW! The lightning blast slammed into the super-cryptid, sending him flying. As the worm writhed violently, Eldon ran to Jordan and grabbed his hand. The two of them were nearly crushed by Corky's great, wobbling body. They dived, dodged, and rolled, finally sprinting out of the chamber and down the long, dark tunnel.

They could hear a horrible thundering noise as

dirt began showering down behind them from Corky's thrashing. All they could do was keep sprinting through the darkness. Every few seconds or so the tunnel would flash brightly, as Corky's lightning butt fired off another blast. Her echoing squeals suddenly dampened as the chamber finally caved in. A massive rush of compressed air forced from the chamber came from behind, blasting Jordan and Eldon off their feet. It shot them out of the tunnel like balls from a giant air rifle.

Jordan and Eldon flew fifty feet through the air and hit the desert ground with a thud. They groaned as they slowly regained their wits.

"Are you all right?" Jordan asked. His friend nodded wearily and gave an A-OK sign with his fingers. Jordan began to laugh. "You're nuts! You just blasted Chupacabra with a fully loaded worm butt!"

"What about you?" Eldon laughed back. "You rodeo-rode the Mongolian Death Worm—*underground*!" The soft rumbling of the cave and tunnel continuing to fall in on itself suddenly got their attention. Eldon looked back in the direction of the underground chamber. "I hope Corky survived. She's clearly under some sort of spell. None of this is her fault."

"What about Chupacabra? He's down there somewhere, too. Shouldn't we go and complete the mission?"

The low, distant rumble grew. The ground shook beneath them. They looked at each other. "I'm thinking it might be best to regroup with the rest of the crew before we investigate," Eldon said.

RRUUMMMMBLLE! The two of them bolted across the Xinjiang desert plain.

Bernard had switched from the jet engines over to the silent rotors, and was flying the Heli-Jet low over the desert.

"This is roughly where you shoved your brother out the door," he said to Abbie, who was seated beside him in the cockpit.

"Thanks for reminding me." She glanced down at the GCPS screen on the console. "Looks like the bracelet is still a mile or so away from here. Let's keep our eyes peeled but follow that tracking device. Hopefully they're with it."

"There!" Morris exclaimed from the window in the passenger hull. "Master, I see two people down below! We just passed them!"

"Good eye, Morris!" Abbie said.

"Turning around," Bernard said. "Prepare for a pickup!"

He circled back over a large indentation in the desert floor.

ZAPOW! The crater split open, and a blast of lightning shot up from the ground, just missing the Heli-Jet. The aircraft rocked as Bernard jerked the controls, tossing Zaya and Morris around in their seats.

"What was that?" Abbie yelled.

"Looked like lightning!" Bernard replied.

"It's Corky!" Zaya was up and out of his seat in seconds. He crowded in behind the pilots. "Did you guys see her? Big worm, about fifty feet long. Hard to miss."

"Just be thankful she missed *us*!" Bernard steadied the Heli-Jet. They were hovering when suddenly something erupted from the sand, opening the split crater further, rising from the ground.

"There she is!" Zaya shouted. "She's okay! Set me down! She needs me!"

"That may not be a wise decision," Morris said gently. He was looking down at the Mongolian Death Worm, who was awkwardly lifting her bulbous head high above the desert floor. "Your creature may have found a new master."

The huge worm steadied itself in a vertical position.

Something scrambled up its blobby, segmented body, then stood atop its head. Chupacabra.

Zaya's eyes narrowed in anger. "That's the mutant cryptid! LEAVE MY CORKY ALONE!"

Abbie and Bernard peered at Chupacabra, standing atop Corky with his glimmering Hydro-Hide and over-sized claw foot . . .

"Forget them!" Abbie said. "Swing back and find Jordan and Eldon—quickly!"

Bernard jerked the controls just as Corky opened her mouth. A thick, green spray of liquid shot from her gaping jaws, missing them by inches.

"What's that monster been feeding my Corky?" Zaya said as the greenish bile flew past the window.

Bernard jerked the controls again, expertly moving them across the sky in retreat. The others were tossed around the cockpit. Morris fell backward into the main cabin, sliding across the floor on his shell.

"Help him up!" Abbie screamed. Zaya rushed over and got him into a seat, inspecting his helmet to make sure it was still tightly attached to his head.

ZAPOW! The tip of Corky's tail shot another light-ning bolt out of the sand, just missing them once more. Bernard banked the aircraft violently.

Abbie turned and looked out the cockpit window. She spotted Eldon and Jordan jumping up and down, just below. "There they are!"

"I'm going in," Bernard said. "Open the sliding door!"

Abbie rushed to the door and jerked it open as Bernard pointed the nose of the Heli-Jet downward. He swooped a few feet above the ground and slowed as the Heli-Jet approached Jordan and Eldon. Abbie and Zaya reached out and grabbed the two of them, pulling them in just as a green spray rained down across the sand. Bernard yanked on the controller. The Heli-Jet whooshed skyward again as Jordan and Eldon scrambled into seats and Abbie slammed the door shut.

As Bernard pulled away from the desert floor and prepared to switch over to the rocket engines, the others looked back to the cracked crater in the distance. Corky was gone, and so was her rider. Zaya was in shock. The Skunk Ape pilot yelled back from the cockpit. "Strap in, everyone! I'm going to full thrust as soon as we get some altitude, but it's going to get a bit bump—"

SMASH! Directly in front of them, the Mongolian Death Worm suddenly exploded out of the desert floor, spraying her green, sandy spit into the sky. Bernard careened out of the way as her gaping mouth snapped at the air in front of them.

Zaya rushed to the window as they narrowly missed

her. "Corky, no! Stop this at once! Bad Death Worm!"

The giant cryptid squealed as she writhed around, her tail charging the air with lightning, her mouth spraying poison across the sky and sand. Bernard maneuvered around Corky's massive head, passing her. Abbie rushed into the cockpit. "You did it, Bernard! Nice piloting!" She turned back to their new passengers. "Are you guys okay?"

Jordan was standing next to Morris, staring at the creature's grinning face beneath his sippy-cup helmet. "Hello," the Kappa said. "My name is Morris."

"Uh, hi," Jordan said.

Zaya approached Jordan and shook his hand. "I'm Zaya," he said. "Corky's Keeper. Sorry about her behavior. This is really out of character for her."

Jordan shook Zaya's hand but continued to stare at Morris. "Hi," he said.

"Preparing the jet engines," Bernard yelled back to them. He was lifting the Heli-Jet higher. "We'll have clearance in just a few more seconds."

Eldon joined Abbie at the cockpit door. "We're not out of this yet." He pointed out the windshield. Ahead in the distance, a small, solitary figure stood on the desert floor, facing them.

"Chupacabra," Abbie said. "Bernard, you'd better get us out of here pronto!"

As the Skunk Ape went to hit the thruster button on the console, Chupacabra slammed his Soil-Sole down on the cracked sand. *KA-THUD!* The ground between him and the rising Heli-Jet buckled like a wave, blasting dirt and dust high into the air. Everything outside the cockpit window turned to a thick, brown fog. The engines made a whining sound as they choked on the thick debris. Then the Heli-Jet went into a tailspin.

Everyone in the cockpit was slammed around as they careened out of control. "Hit the thrusters!" Jordan yelled. "It's our only hope of getting out of here!"

"Are you crazy?" Bernard yelled back. "We don't know which direction we're facing! We could crash!"

"We'll crash if we don't!"

Bernard was panicked. He looked at Eldon. Eldon turned and looked at Abbie. She glanced at everyone, then slammed her hand down on a big red button marked Boost Thrusters.

FWOOOOSH! The Heli-Jet accelerated suddenly, sending everyone but Bernard tumbling backward, slamming into the seats in the main cabin.

The brown, dusty sandstorm had cleared from the cockpit window, and ahead of them on the horizon were the Himalayan Mountains to the south of Xinjiang. "It worked!" Bernard leveled off the Heli-Jet. "I think we're clear!"

Abbie sat up where she had landed in the back of the cabin. She smiled as she heard the others cheering. She began to pull herself up when something rattled beneath one of the seats. She looked down, and her stomach dropped. "Oh, no."

It was Bernard's drink-holder helmet.

"Morris!" Abbie jumped up and ran to the front seat of the cabin. She found the Kappa still strapped in, leaning peacefully against his window. The seat beside him was soaked with water. She peered into the bowl-like sara atop his head. It was empty.

OH NO.

"I'm sorry, master," he said. "I made such a mess. Please forgive me."

Horrified, Abbie glanced down. Morris's feet had already begun to dry out and turn to stone. The effect steadily made its way up his stubby legs. Suddenly, the seat gave way, collapsing like a paper cup beneath his increasing weight. The Heli-Jet jerked.

"What was that?" Bernard said. "What's going on back there?"

The others had gotten up and gathered around.

"Abbie?" Jordan said. "What's wrong with him?"

Abbie had tears in her eyes. "This is all my fault."

RRRRRRRR! The Heli-Jet engines began to whine, and the aircraft violently dropped. Zaya bonked his head on the ceiling. As Bernard struggled to keep them in the air, Eldon ran to the cockpit. Jordan and Abbie stayed close to Morris. She held his head gently and tried to pull him close. He was growing heavier by the second. There was a creak beneath him, as his shell began to turn to stone.

Realizing what was happening, Jordan quickly joined Eldon in the cockpit. He was frantically studying a map readout on the monitor and yelling into the transmitter.

"Mayday! Mayday! Mac, do you read me?" The radio emitted a crackling static. Then they heard a loud voice with a Scottish accent. It was Alistair MacAlister.

"Well, isn't this a sound for sore ears! Where are you fellas?"

"Emergency landing, Mac! We just cleared the foothill pass east of Kathmandu, and we're coming through the other side of the Himalayas, heading south over Bangladesh. Please tell me you guys are still in the area!"

"Aye! Lucky for you ol' Haggis-Breath decided to stop for a snack in the Bay of Bengal! It sounds like you laddies need a place to put that bird down in a hurry! Continue on course due south, and stay low as you come in over the water! I'm sending you coordinates now!"

"Staying low will NOT be a problem," Bernard said as he struggled with the controls. "It feels like we're towing that fat sand-slug!"

ERRRRR! The engines whinnied and shrieked as the Heli-Jet suddenly dropped again. Eldon fumbled with the transmitter as Jordan locked in Alistair's coordinates from the computer, then ran to the main cabin, where he faced Abbie, Zaya, and the almost completely solidified Morris. "Strap in!" he yelled over the straining engine. "Everyone prepare for a crash landing!"

KERSPLASH

12

The Heli-Jet careened low over southern Bangladesh, straight for the tiny, mangrove-covered island that lay just offshore ahead of them. Bernard had cut the engines and was using all his strength to keep the nose of the aircraft up, but Morris had become too heavy for the plane to stay in the air. As they glided in toward impact, Bernard locked down the controls of the Heli-Jet, leaped out of the pilot's chair, and dived into the cabin, protecting the others as best he could with his large, furry body.

The Heli-Jet swooped in, brushing the thick tree-tops that peppered the small island of Sandwip. This helped slow the descending aircraft, but not enough to keep it from clearing the island and hitting the water just beyond it.

KERSPLASH!

The cabin's passengers bounced around wildly as the Heli-Jet skimmed across the calm waters of the Bay of Bengal and immediately began slowly sinking before it even drifted to a stop.

"Quickly! Everyone out!" Eldon's voice called out over the sound of water rushing into the cabin. Jordan and Zaya pulled open the cargo door. The sun was setting in the distance as Eldon helped Zaya through the cabin doorway and into the warm, darkening water outside.

"This might be a good time to tell you that I can't swim," Zaya informed Eldon.

"Of course not," Eldon said, grabbing Zaya around the waist. "You live in the desert with a giant worm. Luckily I have a Badger Badge in Water Rescue. I'll show it to you later. For now, just hold on to me—and kick!" The two of them swam away from the steadily sinking plane.

"Abbie!" Jordan found his sister staring down at water that was pooling and filling from below the seat. Morris was nowhere to be seen. "I have to get out of here!"

"He's gone," she said. "He broke right through and sank like a stone."

Jordan looked down. There was a dark, gaping hole in the floor beneath them. Water was rushing through it at an alarming rate. "You can't stay here! C'mon!" He tugged at his sister, who continued to stare at the floor. The cabin was filling fast. He had his arms around her but couldn't get her to move.

That's when a thick, black-furred arm reached in and pulled the Elite Keepers toward the sliding door.

"C'mon, you two!" Bernard shouted. "Last stop! Everyone off!" He pushed them out the door, then dived down through the hole in the floor.

The warm water of the Bay of Bengal mixed with the cool night air as Jordan struggled to pull Abbie away from the sinking aircraft. Friendly voices shouted out to them through the dim dusk. He looked up to find the Creature Keeper submarine floating just a few hundred feet away.

Suddenly, a shadow darker than the sky swooped past Jordan's head, plucking his sister from his arms, lifting her out of the water. Kriss the Mothman fluttered awkwardly over the deck of the submarine, where he safely set Abbie down before flopping himself nearby like a wet mop.

Jordan climbed the steel ladder and was immediately greeted by Eldon and Zaya on the bridge of the Creature Keepers' submarine. Beside them was a portly older kid with bright orange hair. Even in the dim moonlight, Jordan knew this could only be one person—the Loch Ness Monster's Keeper, Alistair MacAlister.

"Oi! Everyone okay an' accounted fer?"

Besides being soaked, Jordan felt fine. Abbie was standing at the edge of the deck staring out at the dark water as the top of the Heli-Jet disappeared. Beside her was the West Virginian Mothman. Kriss and Abbie shared a special bond, and while Jordan sometimes felt it a bit creepy, right now Jordan was glad he was there with her.

"What's all this, then?" Alistair shouted out. "It's no time to pout—yer lucky to be alive! You folks just barely survived a crash landing!"

"Not all of us," Abbie said softly, gazing out at the still water.

"Aye, the Kappa," Alistair said softly as he approached Abbie. "Y'know, that creature always reminded me of the wee snappin' turtles we have back home on Loch Ness. They're slow as death when they're floppin' around on land like little doorstoppers. But the thing about 'em is, once you get 'em back in the water—whoosh! Off they go, full of life again!"

Abbie looked up at this strange redheaded Keeper. Alistair was grinning ear to ear. She looked at the others. Bernard, Eldon, Zaya, her brother, they all stood there soaked to the bone, but they were smiling, too.

Alistair put two chubby fingers in his mouth and whistled loudly.

"SKRONK!"

The green and graceful head of the Loch Ness Monster lifted out of the water. Her young Hydro-Hide scales sparkled in the moonlight as her back rose up alongside the submarine deck. Abbie slowly approached. Her eyes went wide. Sitting atop Nessie was Morris, his sara refilled with water from the Bay of Bengal. He waved to her as Nessie gently slid him along her tail, safely delivering him on board.

"Morris!" Abbie hugged the cryptid tightly. "I was so worried you were gone! I'm so sorry! I'll never let anything happen to you again!"

Morris smiled and hugged her back. "I did as you asked, master. I took responsibility for myself, and filled my own sara! See?" He began to bow deeply.

"NO!" Everyone shouted out as Abbie quickly righted him.

"No bowing! You'll spill again!" She laughed through her tears. "Morris, do you see what this means? You filled your own bowl! You can start thinking for yourself!"

Morris contemplated this for a moment, then broke out into a wide grin. "Yes! And I am now thinking for myself how happy I am that you are still my master, master!"

"Okay. We'll work on that one." Abbie gave him a big hug.

The tiny island of Sandwip lay just off the southern coast of Bangladesh. It was populated mostly by quiet fishermen who lived near the center of the island to avoid the threat of storms and floods—as well as all the loud screeching. The mangrove trees that grew along the beach at the southern tip of the island were populated with howler monkeys, who were not quiet at all. They were like a living intruder alert system for the inland locals of Sandwip, keeping a loud lookout for strangers approaching from the sea.

On this moonlit night, those howling alarms had a lot to sound off about. The odd-looking trespassers who walked onto their beach were definitely not locals. First the monkeys screeched at the chubby, red-haired boy in a kilt. They then shrieked at four tired-looking, drenched kids. They hooted at the largest turtle they'd ever seen. Their ruckus grew louder and wilder, right up until they spotted the last member of the group. As the giant, smelly, black-furred ape king casually strolled out of the bay, the monkeys decided maybe they'd give it a rest and call it a night.

Alistair hooked the Heli-Jet to the submarine, eventually towing it toward the shore. Then Bernard, with a big push from Nessie, was able to get it up on the beach for a full inspection. The damage was substantial. As Bernard and Kriss went to work trying to patch it up and get it running again, Morris splashed and played in the waves. Alistair joined the other humans on the beach for an emergency Creature Keeper campfire conference.

Jordan was the only one not seated by the fire. After drying his belongings (first and foremost his grandfather's journal), he sat on the sand away from the others, searching the pages of the old book for something he desperately wanted to find.

Abbie had already found what she was looking for in *her* book, and she read to the others from *Raising and Caring for Your Kappa*. "Water is the life force of your Kappa," she read. "Take great caution to keep his sara filled at all times, for he will turn to solid stone whenever it runs empty. Be sure to take extra care that your Kappa's sara is not depleted more than twice between the First Quarter moons—upon the third occurrence within one lunar cycle, the Kappa will remain in a stone state forever."

"Twice the First Quarter, third within the second cycle, *ack!*" Alistair said. "Sounds like math. I'm horrible at math."

"It isn't that complicated, Mac," Eldon said. He was drying his Badger Badge sash, holding it over the fire with a stick. "Morris can't spill his hat three times within the lunar month that falls between First Quarter moons. If he does, he's toast."

"Ten-ton toast," Zaya added.

"That's some heavy toast," Alistair said.

"Number one was when his own keepers emptied it," Eldon said. "And I'm afraid it still counts."

"And number two, which nearly killed us all, was under my protection." Abbie stared sadly into the fire.

"Hey, I'm the one who messed up," Eldon said to her. "It was reckless of me to ask Shika and Katsu to empty Morris's sara. I thought it was the best way to keep him safe, and I didn't know what else to do."

"Well, if I hadn't gone there and reanimated him, he'd be home safe, sound, and solid!" Abbie's eyes flickered in the firelight.

"I don't blame you for reanimating him, Abbie. I should've explained what you were going to find in that Japanese forest." He checked his sash for dampness and slipped it back on. "Of course, in my defense, you were about to toss me out of a moving Heli-Jet."

"Can't we turn Morris to stone and hide him on this island for now?" Zaya asked.

Abbie shook her head. "He's spilled twice within the lunar cycle. If he spills again before the next First Quarter moon, we won't be able to bring him back again."

There was a long silence as Abbie stared into the

fire. Zaya scooted closer to her. "Don't blame yourself," he said. "Blame Chupacabra. He got to my creature, too. He's behind all of this. He's the one we have to work together to take down, for the safety of all the cryptids."

"Zaya's right," Eldon said. "He's up to something. Look at this." He held up a small vial. Inside was a dollop of green goo. "I scraped this sample from Corky's teeth while she slept. By its stinky footlike odor, I'd say it's a very rare Siberian valerian root extract. It's particularly effective on cryptids. It induces a dreamlike state where the creature thinks it's asleep but isn't. Under this spell, a cryptid could be made to do pretty much anything it's told." He held up another vial. It contained the same color goo. "This I got off the side of the Heli-Jet before it sank. It's what Corky was spitting at us. Same stuff. Chupacabra must have given her the powder, then had her regurgitate it out of her spray glands. We were lucky Bernard was able to fly us out of there without being hit. But please don't tell him I said that. It'll go to his head."

A revving sound from the shore got everyone's attention. Bernard yelled to them as the rotors on the Heli-Jet began to spin. "Hey! Look who got the chopper running!"

Kriss was happily but awkwardly fluttering behind

the exhaust valve when a smoky explosion suddenly blasted from the jet, covering him in wet soot. The rotors jerked to a halt. Bernard looked up at the Mothman. "Uh, never mind!" he said.

Alistair stood up. "Never send a Mothman or a Skunk Ape to do a Keeper's job. I'll go and give them a hand before they blow up the island."

"Hold up, Mac," Eldon said. "Those wandering cryptids you've been out here returning to their

Keepers—any chance they'd been exposed to this root powder?"

"I don't think so," Alistair said. "These creatures have been wanderin' off from this whole stretch of coastline around the Indian Ocean, from eastern Africa to northwestern Australia. Me, Kriss, and Haggis-Breath had just returned the Sumatran Golden Liger to her Keeper when we got your distress call. Dumb pussycat was just standing on the tip of Sumatra, staring across at this very bay, plain as day for any and all to see! Good thing cats hate water, or I betcha she woulda jumped."

"What was she looking for?" Abbie asked.

"Danged if I know," Alistair said. "She'd traveled miles, just to stand and stare. When I found her, it was like she didn't know me. But she wasn't sleepwalking like you said. She was just fixated on something on the horizon. Like somethin' I couldn't hear was callin' to her. Then, all of a sudden, it was as if whatever it was just stopped. She snapped right out of it. Didn't know where she was or how she got there."

"That doesn't sound like the aftereffects of valerian-root powder," Eldon said. "Where is she now? I'd like to examine her."

"We got her home safe. Nessie and me laid a nice

hoax down at the beach to throw off any folks who might've spotted her, and Kriss flew her back to her Keeper. I tell ya this, thank goodness for those tracking devices of Jordan's. We'd have a real problem on our hands without 'em!"

Jordan didn't respond. He was still lost in his grandfather's journal.

"Anyway," Alistair continued, "it's been the same with all the cryptids we've tracked down. Funny thing is, whether they're on the move or standin' and starin,' we find 'em all fixed in the same direction." Mac stood up and pointed north, back through the torn path in the trees that was cut down by the Heli-Jet's emergency landing. He turned and trudged off in the opposite direction, toward Bernard and the others trying to repair the aircraft at the shore.

"There's no way Chupacabra isn't somehow connected to all this," Abbie said.

"That's right," said Eldon. "We need to figure out a way to trap him. Without him trapping us again, that is."

"I don't think it's a smart idea, heading back to that desert. He and Corky are too powerful."

"But how are we going to trap him if we don't go back?" Eldon said.

"Easy." Jordan finally spoke up. "We go where we know he's going to show up next." He held up the journal so they could all see. On the page was a drawing Grampa Grimsley had sketched years ago.

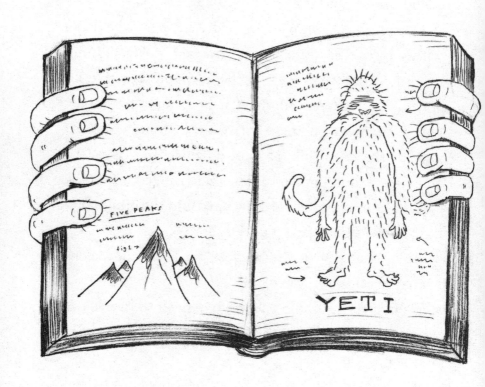

13

As Bernard, Kriss, and Alistair worked through the night repairing the waterlogged Heli-Jet, Zaya slept buried up to his neck in the sand under a nearby mangrove tree, while Morris floated peacefully by the shore, bobbing in the bay water. Jordan, Abbie, and Eldon huddled by the dwindling fire as Jordan shared with them what he'd pieced together.

"There was something Chupacabra said down in that wormhole. I've been reading through Grampa Grimsley's journal to try to find some answers. Chupacabra has a big plan up his stolen sleeves. Something called Operation Pangaea. And he's trying to harness the power of the Perfect Storm to achieve it."

"What's the Perfect Storm?" Abbie said.

Eldon removed his hat and scratched his head. "I hope it doesn't mean what I think it means. The worst-case scenario. The combined force of all three elemental powers, collected under the control of a single cryptid."

"He's well on his way," Abbie said. "Chupacabra has Nessie's Hydro-Hide, which can manipulate water. Then he stole one of Syd's Soil-Soles, allowing him to disrupt earth and rock. The third belongs to the Yeti. A blizzard beard, or something?"

"Blizzard-*Bristles*," Eldon said. "Potentially the most dangerous one of all, especially in the wrong hands. Or in this case, under the wrong nose. The Yeti's great mustache is made up of Blizzard-Bristles, through which he controls wind and weather. Swiping that from the Yeti would be a near-impossible task. But if he were somehow able to, Chupacabra would control the three elemental powers. He'd have them all."

"Not quite," Jordan said. "According to Chupacabra, there's a fourth."

"What?" Abbie said. "What's the power? And which creature?"

"He didn't elaborate."

"This is news to me," Eldon said, "and very troubling. But if it's true, it could explain why all these cryptids are going AWOL. Chupacabra may somehow be luring them out of hiding to find the one who possesses the fourth power."

"If you don't know, then no one does," Abbie said. She rested her gaze on Morris, who was still floating peacefully in the lapping water. "And if it's been kept secret even from the Creature Keepers, it could belong to a creature no one would ever expect."

"Wait," Eldon said to Jordan. "If there are *two* more special cryptids out there, what makes you so sure Chupacabra will go for the Yeti next?"

"Because he didn't kill me, even though he still thinks I'm Grampa Grimsley. In fact, it's *because* he thinks I'm Grampa Grimsley that I'm alive. He said I was the only one who could lead him to where it is, and if I didn't remember or cooperate, he'd drag me to the top of the world, and we'd work our way down, searching for him."

"Top of the world?" Eldon said.

"Mount Everest," Abbie said. "The highest mountain on earth." She turned to Eldon. "That's the Yeti's hangout, right? The Abominable Snowman, all that stuff? Everyone knows that!"

119

"I don't know that," Eldon said. "At least, not for sure."

"What do you mean? Knowing that is your thing!"

"Besides Chupacabra, the Yeti was the only other cryptid who refused your grandfather's help and protection. Today he sits all alone with the elemental power of his Blizzard-Bristles, keeping the wind and weather in balance. But I'm afraid Chupacabra wasn't lying—your grandfather was the only one who knew the whereabouts of Wilford."

"*Wilford?*" Abbie exclaimed. "Who names these guys?"

Jordan held up the journal. "Grampa Grimsley wrote about nearly every creature he discovered. All his observations, everything he learned about them. But according to this, there was only one creature he learned *from*. And all he says is he met him somewhere in the Himalayan Mountains."

Abbie scoffed. "That's like saying he's in the ocean. The Himalayas are huge! There must be something Grampa Grimsley wrote down in that old book that could give us a clue. What did he mean he learned *from* the Yeti?"

Jordan opened the journal and began to read a passage written by his grandfather:

This great creature has shown me my path and pointed me toward my destiny. I have so much more to learn from him, but he will not let me stay with him up here, and he refuses to come down. I did not understand at first, but now I see that as I am destined to go out and help the others, he is destined to remain here alone— one on the mountain, one with the mountain – FOREVER!

"But which mountain?" Abbie said. "We can't do what Chupacabra's doing and start at the highest peak and work our way down!"

"Wait," Jordan said. "That's it!"

"That's what?"

"That's where we can find him—Everest!"

"Seems unlikely," Eldon said. "Nowadays, Everest is one of the most climbed mountains in the world. How can you be so sure that's where the Yeti lives?"

"Because he told me!"

Eldon looked at Jordan with some concern. "Okay. I think maybe you bumped your head when we crash-landed. Jordan, you never had a conversation with the Yeti."

"Not the Yeti," Abbie said. "He means Chupacabra!" She and Jordan were both on their feet. "You're right! We don't have to find Wilford. We just have to find Chupacabra before *he* finds Wilford!"

"What?" Eldon said.

"Exactly!" Jordan said. "And the first place he's going to look is where he told me he would—the top of the world!"

Jordan and Abbie grinned at each other as they said in unison: "Mount Everest!"

Eldon stared at the both of them. "Is it okay if I'm totally confused?"

* * *

As day broke over the Bay of Bengal, the howler monkeys sat silently in the treetops, watching the strange visitors hug and say good-bye to one another. Alistair MacAlister boarded the submarine so that he, Kriss, and Nessie could make one more pass for wandering cryptids. Eldon and Jordan thanked him for helping Bernard fix the Heli-Jet.

"My pleasure," Alistair said. "Her rockets are on their last legs and won't run at full capacity, but the chopper rotors work, and she should still blast at a good clip."

"I hope so," Eldon said. "Bernard and Zaya are flying her up to Siberia. That's where Chupacabra likely collected that rare, potent strain of valerian root. I need them to get a specimen, then fly it back to the CKCC and get it to Katsu."

"That creep?" Abbie said. "What's he going to do, scowl at it?"

"Katsu is a serious young man," Eldon said. "But he's also an excellent botanist. If he were an actual Badger Ranger, he'd easily be eligible for a First-Class Badger Badge in Herbology, just like the one I have." Eldon shoved his sash in their faces, showing off a tiny, leaf-adorned patch. "See the little leaf there?"

"Somehow Katsu doesn't strike me as the Badger

Ranger type," Jordan said.

"Well, he'll be able to break down the dangerous root's properties and come up with an antidote for Corky, which is what matters," Eldon said.

Moments later, the rotors to the Heli-Jet fired up, lifting Bernard and Zaya off the beach. They waved from the cockpit window as they cleared the mangrove trees and headed north. Jordan, Abbie, and Eldon then turned and waved good-bye in the other direction as Alistair closed the hatch on the submarine and Nessie winked at them. But Kriss lingered behind on the beach.

"You can't come with us," Abbie told the Mothman. "We're traveling upriver in broad daylight, where there may be a lot of people. You could be spotted."

"She's right," Eldon added. "Besides, you'll be more help to Mac in locating and returning any wandering cryptids. You need to get to the bottom of what's making them act that way. Whatever's causing it, I'm convinced it's not the valerian root."

Kriss nodded. He gave Abbie a shy smile, then flapped his great wings and zoomed into the air, following after Nessie and Alistair.

Jordan, Abbie, and Eldon stood on the sand. Bobbing in the water before them was a sad little skiff they were planning on borrowing from one of the village fishermen. Farther out in the water, Morris happily swam around, darting through the waves, splashing and playing in the water.

As the Heli-Jet faded over the horizon and the submarine disappeared beneath the deep waters of the bay, Jordan looked down at the rickety little boat. "Sure would've been easier to get a lift from either of those guys to the base of Everest."

Abbie secured a rope to the front of the skiff and pulled it tight. "If Morris spills one more time before the First Quarter moon, he'll permanently turn to stone. I can't risk flying him in the air again. You're welcome to travel with us by river or stay here and live among the monkeys. Your call."

Eldon was checking his official Badger Ranger pocket atlas. "Across the bay to the west is the mouth of the Meghna River. That merges into the Padma River, which will take us straight up through the heart of Bangladesh. It splits with the Brahmaputra River near the Indian border, but if we stay on the Padma, it becomes the famous Ganges River and crosses into India. Then we then hit the Kosi, which will get us close enough to hike in to the base of Everest. You ready to do this, Elite Keepers?"

"Sure," Jordan said. "It's only about five hundred miles, almost entirely upriver and against the current. Oh, and our little boat has no motor."

Abbie took up the other end of the rope and tied it into a loose leash. She smiled at Morris, who was shooting in and out of the waves like a torpedo.

"Who says we don't have a motor?"

The local fishermen along the Meghna River stared in wonderment at the little skiff as it whizzed past them upstream at an alarming rate. The two boys rowing the narrow boat didn't look like especially strong rowers— certainly not strong enough to warrant how quickly their skiff zipped past and around the bend.

Once clear of the onlookers, Jordan and Eldon pulled the oars inside and sat back, enjoying the ride. Abbie sat in the front, manning a taut rope. She gave it a short tug.

The other end of the rope appeared in front of the boat. It was tied around Morris's thick neck. As he effortlessly pulled them up the river, he spun around into a backstroke and grinned up at Abbie. He gobbled down a mouthful of tiny hilsa fish.

"How am I doing, master? Do you have any instructions for me?"

"You're doing great, Morris," Abbie said. "We're approaching a village, so keep underwater and out of sight. And remember, just go with the flow!"

"Technically, we're asking him to go *against* the flow," Eldon said.

"It's just an expression, dorkface. I'm trying to teach him independence."

"With a leash around his neck?"

Morris squirted a stream of water over Abbie's head and directly into Jordan's face.

"Hey!" Jordan wiped it off angrily. "You did that on purpose!"

"Nice shot, Morris," Abbie said. "You'd better keep your head down now."

"As you wish, master!" Morris smiled and submerged, pulling the skiff up to the fishing village of Chandpur. Just beyond the little town, the river forked in two different directions. While Jordan and Abbie went out to get food, water, and supplies, Eldon consulted his pocket atlas. By the time the Grimsleys had returned and loaded up the boat, Eldon had charted the next leg of their journey. "That's the Padma River," he said, pointing to the narrower of the two waterways that lay ahead. "It'll take us northwest into India. Abbie, please let our little outboard engine know that's where we want to go."

As Eldon and Jordan picked up their oars, Abbie yanked on Morris's rope. The skiff suddenly jolted away from the dock. Then she yanked the rope to one side like a horse's rein, and they veered toward the mouth of the Padma River.

Hours passed as they made their way toward the border with India. Turning a wide bend, they all suddenly looked to the distant horizon and fell silent. Mount Everest looked as if it was floating, like some massive mother ship hovering above the earth's surface, trying to find a parking spot.

The three Creature Keepers steadily continued to wind their way upriver in their Kappa-propelled little boat. Jordan leaned over the side, dragging his hand through the cool water. He stared at his reflection in the river, then turned to Eldon, who had taken the reins and was holding Morris's line at the front of the skiff. "Eldon, do you think my grandfather came by way of this same river?"

"It's certainly possible," Eldon said. "He sure didn't come by Heli-Jet."

Abbie was lying lazily at the rear of the boat with her leg dangling over the side, her bare toes dipping in and out of the water. Jordan glanced back at her, then continued. "I wish this river could tell us. I wish Nessie's Hydro-Hide could communicate with the waters of the world, not just control them. Maybe between the rivers, seas, and oceans, we'd discover if he was still out there somewhere."

After a moment, Eldon spoke up. "To the people who have lived in this part of the world for generations, these rivers are considered sacred. They're alive, with memories that stretch along as far as they do, flowing not just through land, but across time. These rivers remember every passenger they carried, and recognize those who return to them."

Abbie lifted her head. She and Jordan stared at Eldon for a moment. He pointed to a patch on his sash. "Badger Badge in Sub-Himalayan Cultures."

Jordan rested his head against a pack of supplies and felt the water flowing through his fingertips. He stared off at the hazy white peak of Everest in the distance and felt his eyelids growing heavier. He lifted his head and glanced back. Abbie was sound asleep, her foot still dragging in the water. Jordan settled his head down again and stared toward the front of the boat. "You okay up there, Eldon?"

"You betcha," Eldon replied. "It's been a long couple of days and we don't know what lies ahead. You'd better get some shut-eye now, while you can."

Jordan breathed in the cool, early evening air as he continued to stare at Everest's brilliant white peak, painted against the darkening sky. He counted the first few stars that twinkled to life around it, then slipped into a deep sleep.

Light flickered against Jordan's eyelids, flashing him out of a sound slumber. He opened his eyes. A patchwork of banyan tree branches stretched overhead, the morning sunlight streaming through the fluttering leaves and onto his face.

He sat up. Both Eldon and Abbie were asleep. Beyond them, small mountains loomed in the distance, but none of them looked familiar. None of them looked like they were floating on the horizon. None of them were Mount Everest.

"Oh, no." Jordan scanned their immediate surroundings. They were still on a river. The boat rocked as he scrambled to the front, where Eldon stirred, the rope loosely hanging in his relaxed hand. Jordan looked past him, off the bow of the boat. "Morris," he yelled. "MORRIS, WHERE ARE YOU?"

"Good morning!" Morris's friendly voice suddenly sounded from off the side of the boat. "Did you all have a peaceful rest?" He was swimming alongside them.

"Morris! Where are we? Where's Everest?"

"What's going on?" Eldon sat up groggily.

"Everest is gone," Jordan said. "We lost it."

Abbie was up and looking around at the rear of the boat. "It's the biggest mountain in the world. How could we lose it?"

"Oh, gosh," Eldon said. "I must have fallen asleep at the wheel." Abbie rushed to the side of the boat. Morris was floating along, quite content. "Oh, Morris," she said. "What did you do?"

"I did just as you instructed, master," he said, flipping onto his back and staring up at the tree branches overhead. "I went with the flow!"

They were drifting with a current, but couldn't tell which direction. Eldon had his compass out. He tapped it and checked again. "Strange," he said. "We're still heading north. How could we be floating downstream, but heading toward the mountains?"

They began drifting faster as the patchwork of banyan tree branches overhead grew thicker. It soon became a tunnel of twisting limbs. The current picked up, and so did the speed of their little skiff.

Jordan held on to the boat along with Eldon and Abbie as they began to cruise faster than Morris had ever towed them. The river was rushing now, growing rougher, and descending between towering natural walls of stone on either side. The little skiff was barreling through some sort of river canyon, careening deeper and deeper, picking up speed by the second.

"Whee!" Morris was cruising alongside them on his shell, splashing and skimming through the rushing rapids like he was on a water-park ride.

"Morris! Help us stop! Grab hold of the boat and slow us down!"

FLOOSH! The channel suddenly dropped them into a steep natural flume. Their tiny skiff bottomed out into a large underground pool that diverted the whitewater, slowing the mad current into a gentle swirling whirlpool. Morris and the little boat spun off and drifted to rest at a mossy stone embankment.

Jordan, Abbie, and Eldon sat up. They looked around and took in the walls of a deep canyon rising up all around them.

"Hee-hee! That was fun!" Morris's laugh echoed within the underground chamber as he floated alongside the boat.

"What the heck are you laughing about?" Jordan said. "Can't you see what you've done? You've taken us completely off course!"

"Don't talk to him like that," Abbie said. "He just did what we asked him to!"

"I think we all should calm down," Eldon said.

"Are you kidding?" Jordan snapped back at him. "This is *your* fault! How could you fall asleep at the wheel and leave our destiny in the hands of that oversized tadpole?"

"Golly, Jordan. I am sorry, but that's uncalled for."

"You're being a total jerk, Jordan!" Abbie looked at Morris. "Don't listen to him!"

"Hello there!" Morris smiled back. "I'm Morris. Pleased to make your acquaintances. What are your names?"

"He's lost his waterlogged mind," Jordan said. "This actually explains a lot."

"Morris," Abbie said gently. "You know our names."

"I am not addressing you, master." Morris pointed past them.

Jordan, Abbie, and Eldon spun around. Standing on the embankment were two short, bald, elderly men with long white beards, each wearing a robe.

"Hello," one of the little men said. "If you please, which of you is responsible for navigating this modest vessel here?"

The three Creature Keepers slowly turned back to look at Morris, who was floating on his back. He spit a spout of water into the air and giggled.

The little man added: "You see, one cannot navigate oneself here. Only those destined to find Banyan Canyon discover it."

"Morris," Abbie said gently. "How did you steer us here?"

"I just did as you said, master. I went with the flow."

The Kanchenjungan mountain monks did not live, in fact, *on* Mount Kanchenjunga. They lived somewhat beneath it, within deep, slotted canyons that made up a hidden, maze-like moat of rock and underground pools at the southern base of the mountain.

This series of secret crevices formed a cathedral of mossy, fern-covered rock walls looming high overhead. Golden sunlight cascaded through the canyons, reflecting off crystal-clear pools and rivulets carved into the stone floor. The rays cast a liquid light show on the walls, transforming the deep catacombs into a twinkling, magical underground world.

And Jordan was so over it.

"Sorry to be rude. It's a lovely place you guys have

here, but we really must be going. If you could just show us the exit, we'll be out of your—er, hair."

Jordan was met with blank, peaceful stares from the pair of monks who greeted them, as well as the dozen or so similarly dressed, similarly bald monks who had joined them.

Jordan turned to more familiar faces. "You wanna help me out here, guys?"

Eldon and Abbie sat on small, smooth rocks around a large, table-sized formation in the floor, while Morris floated in a nearby natural pool of crystal-clear water. Two of the mountain monks served them tea, as another turned to Jordan.

"Please, sit. You are our guests. All will work itself out in due time."

"No, see, it won't," Jordan snapped back. "Because this mountain we're under, it's the *wrong mountain*. We're supposed to be climbing Everest by now. *Mount Everest*? Heard of it? But we're stuck under this stupid mountain nobody's ever heard of—"

"Mount Kanchenjunga," one of the other monks gently informed him.

"Whatever! My point is no one cares because it's not Everest! And it's who-knows-how-many-miles from—"

"Eighty," Eldon said, holding up his pocket atlas.

"*Eighty* miles from where we need to be! So thank

you very much, but if we don't make it to Everest, we'll run out of time!"

The monk smiled at him. "Far better to run out of time on the wrong path, so that you may find time to wander upon the right one."

He handed Jordan a cup of tea. Jordan stared back, then looked over at Eldon and Abbie. "Am I the only one who isn't completely insane right now?"

They casually sipped from their cups. "We should really tell him," Eldon said.

"I dunno," Abbie sighed. "It's pretty fun watching him freak out."

"Tell me what?" Jordan said. "SOMEONE TELL ME WHAT'S GOING ON!"

"Turn around, dorkface," Abbie said. "And try not to hurt yourself."

Jordan turned. On the large, smooth rock wall behind him was a carving. Jordan recognized it immediately.

"Oh. Okay. That's the, uh . . ."

"The Yeti," one of the mountain monks said. "Do you know him?"

"Me? Haven't had the pleasure, no. So he's . . . is he in?"

All the monks suddenly glanced at one another, then began to frantically search about. They looked behind each other, checked inside their robe pockets, peeked under tiny rocks. "Good heavens," one of them said. "We've misplaced the Yeti again!" They all burst out laughing. Eldon and Abbie joined in.

"Okay, very funny," Jordan said. "He isn't here. I get it. Stupid question."

"No, no, he's here," the monk said. "He just lives upstairs." Jordan, Abbie, and Eldon all looked up the wall with the cave painting on it, stretching high and away above them. "Like, *way* upstairs. Come. I will show you."

A few monks led Jordan, Abbie, Eldon, and Morris through the slot canyons, deeper into the heart of Mount Kanchenjunga. The Kappa was careful not to spill his sari as they reached a humid cavern where more monks sat around, chatting happily and enjoying the steamy air.

"What are your names?" Abbie finally asked her guides.

"We do not have names," one of the monks said.

"Names are labels, for things. We are not things. We simply . . . are."

"We have to call you something. If you did have a name, what would it be?"

He contemplated for a moment. "I've always thought 'Jagger' would be cool."

"Wow," Eldon said. "Jagger, this place is incredible."

"And no one knows you guys are here?" Jordan said.

The monk not named Jagger gently shook his head. "Mount Kanchenjunga is the second tallest mountain in the Himalayas, after Everest. As you said, few have heard of number two, and few care. Which is nice for us. Those who fixate on the biggest and the strongest sometimes miss what is special about the meek."

Abbie smiled at this and glanced at Morris, who grinned contentedly.

"Jagger," Eldon said. "It's critical that we see the Yeti. We're Creature Keepers."

Jordan leaned close and showed off his golden badge. "*Elite* Creature Keepers."

"Yeah, we figured. It's why we let you in."

"You saw the badge?" Jordan asked.

"No. Not everyone travels around with the Japanese Kappa. Also, you bear a resemblance to a Keeper I knew many years ago. Come."

The monk not named Jagger crossed the cavern

floor and led them to a set of steps leading up to a circular altar carved out of the stone wall. Decorating the walls around it were more carvings similar to the one of the Yeti, but much more detailed. These carvings told a story. And the monk not named Jagger began to tell it.

"We are now directly beneath the heart of Mount Kanchenjunga, a holy mountain protected for centuries by our ancestors." He pointed to various symbols, all surrounded by a large pyramid shape representing the mountain. "Kanchenjunga means 'the five treasures of the high snow,' which the early worshippers considered to be gold, silver, gems, grain, and sacred texts. As other tribes heard of these treasures, they threatened to climb and loot the mountain. So a myth was created to frighten people away—the Rakshasa, or Kanchenjunga Demon, was a fearsome beast who protected these treasures." He pointed to a crude but scary-looking Yeti-like character carved atop the pyramid. "Of course, like many myths, the Rakshasa was based on something half real."

"So there's a real demon creature up there," Abbie said.

"Demon, no. Creature, yes." The monk pointed to the next carving. A Yeti symbol stood atop a new pyramid, with four smaller peaks, two jutting up from either side. Eldon stared up at it as the monk continued. "He'd always been there, as long as anyone could remember. But not to protect any treasure, or even the mountain. In our legends, the Yeti *is* the mountain. He is the ice and snow. The wind, the weather. He is part of Mount Kanchenjunga, and it is a part of him. They are one and the same."

"Are the five treasures half true, too?" Jordan said. "Like, two and a half treasures?"

"No." Eldon was still staring up at the five pyramids that symbolized the Kanchenjunga mountain range. "Look. The five treasures of the high snow."

"Please, I'm telling a story. It's a bit rude to jump ahead." The monk continued to tell his story. "Over the centuries, people forgot about old myths. Climbing and conquering became the desire of man. Luckily for my people, there was a bigger treasure to be had, which lay a safe distance west of here." The carving showed small stick figures lined before a much bigger mountain. "Eighty miles to the west," Jordan said. "Everest."

The last carving showed the five peaks again, with smaller stick figures inside of the central one, and the Yeti atop it.

"Then came us, the mountain monks. Gatekeepers to Mount Kanchenjunga. From beneath its deepest base we protected its highest peak. No one was allowed to pass. And no human hand has ever touched its crown."

Jordan pointed to a lone, carved stick figure above the line of monks, halfway up the central mountain. "What about that guy? Who's this?"

"He is the one you remind me of. The one human who proved himself worthy to pass. He climbed to the top of Mount Kanchenjunga. Like you, he found his way to Banyan Canyon because he was destined to come here. He called himself an explorer, although he did not know what it was he was seeking. He had made a terrible mistake. He was running away from that mistake, but had grown tired of running. And so he stopped here. He lived with us and embraced our ways. He learned to trust us, and soon, himself. And that's when he was granted access to the treasures of the high snow."

Jordan studied the carvings that told the story he was hearing. As he listened to the monk, he felt a strange excitement awaken in his chest.

"The young explorer was sent up Mount Kanchen-junga with one simple rule—that he stop short of conquering her peak. The very top of the mountain was to remain sacred, untouched by humans. He gave his word, and once he reached the top, he kept that word. He did not know it, but this was his final test. The test of humility. Not many men could resist such a conquest. But this man was special. And that is why he won the final trust of the one he did not realize he was seeking."

"The Yeti," Eldon whispered.

Jordan's heart was beating faster. He watched as Abbie asked the exact question he was thinking. "This explorer," she said. "What was his name?"

The Kanchenjungan mountain monk smiled. "I believe you both already know the answer to that question."

Jordan said it aloud first. "George Grimsley."

The mountain monk not named Jagger smiled gently. "*Duh*," he said.

Morris made soft gurgling sounds as the monk patted him on his head. "You are pure of heart and have the wisdom of the earth, my dear creature. But it was not you who brought your friends here."

"Then who did?" Eldon asked.

"I believe it was Kanchenjunga herself who summoned you. She asked the rivers to direct you to her, the currents to deliver you. And so, here you are."

Standing near the altar, they turned around to see all the other monks on their feet, staring at them in silence. The monk not named Jagger gestured toward the stone steps. "Grandchildren of George Grimsley, you two may pass."

The silent monks bowed their heads in unison as

Jordan and Abbie slowly climbed the steps. Abbie stopped halfway. "Wait," she said. "Morris is my responsibility. I won't leave him alone again."

"Of course," the monk said. "Our rules are made by men, for men. This cryptid is a sacred creature, free to come and go as he pleases."

Morris looked at Abbie. "Master?" he said. "What would you have me do?"

Abbie smiled at him. "Do what you want to do," she said. Morris grinned and ran toward her, excitedly sloshing some of the water out of his bowl. "Whoa," Abbie said. "But let's try not to spill, okay? Kind of a rule."

Jordan turned back to face Eldon. The First-Class Badger Ranger forced a smile as he raised his hand in a Badger claw salute. "Don't worry about me, Elite Keepers. I'll hold down the fort here at base camp! You get up there and protect that cryptid!"

The mountain monk handed Jordan and Abbie heavy coats. "Yak wool," he said. "Nice and toasty." He led Jordan, Abbie, and Morris into the round chamber. It was actually a shaft that led straight up, disappearing beyond what Jordan could see, into darkness. A chilly breeze came from above. He and Abbie pulled their coats on.

The monk lifted a small mallet. "Remember,

please—not a single human toe on the peak." He swung the mallet and struck a bell that hung within a hollowed cutout in the stone wall beside the round room. The tone reverberated all around them, echoing throughout the chamber and over their heads. Jordan, Abbie, and Morris stood in the center and peered upward into the dark shaft as the tone vibrated, louder and faster.

As the last vibrations from the bell faded, snowflakes began gently drifting down the dark shaft. Morris giggled as he stuck out his tongue to catch them. A whistling sound grew louder high above them as a blast of mountain air rushed down, washing over them. The gust picked up, swirling the light snow dust all around their feet, waists, shoulders, and heads.

The snow was soon whipping around them, thicker and faster. Through the moving wall of white, Jordan could barely make out Eldon's silhouette. He pulled his yak-wool coat tightly around him.

WHOOSH! In an instant, Jordan's feet left the ground. He, Abbie, and Morris flew straight up the shaft, spinning higher and higher in the billowing spiral of the dark, snowy cyclone. They shot up at an incredible pace until they finally reached daylight, flying out the top, bursting into the thin, cold mountain air.

Jordan landed headfirst in a snowbank. He pulled himself out and spit a mouthful of snow. The wind had stopped whirling, and all was calm and silent, muffled by the thick snow covering everything. He stood up and looked around. He was standing on the top of the highest summit, looking out at the four lower peaks of Mount Kanchenjunga. "The five treasures," he said to himself. This wasn't Mount Everest, but he felt like he'd arrived at the top of the world.

"Morris!" Jordan turned toward the sound of Abbie's voice. She was yelling from a few yards away. As she waded through a snowbank near a small grove of evergreen trees, Jordan ran to her. "I can't find him," she said, upset and frightened. "What if he spilled his sara again! If he turns to stone, this time he can't be changed back!"

"I'm sure he's okay," Jordan said. "He could've landed anywhere. Keep looking!"

The air was freezing as they searched. They approached a snow-covered outcropping and heard a soft yelp pierce the still air. Abbie ran toward it. She circled the rock and trudged higher along a path leading upward, running faster, until—

"Abbie, *no!*" She froze in her tracks. He caught up to her and pointed at her feet. "Look."

The path before them ran straight to the peak of

Mount Kanchenjunga—a ledge that stopped at nothing but sky. The snow between that crest and where they stood was pristine, whiter than white, sparkling in the sunlight. Untouched by man.

Another Kappa squeal sounded out, from just over the ledge. "I know we promised, but I have to go," Abbie said. She went to take a step onto the pure snow, when a shadow fell over them both. Something large appeared at the top ledge, blocking out the sunlight. It slowly lifted its arms and held over its head the unmistakable silhouette of a half shell.

"Morris!" Abbie cried. The shadow-beast leaped toward them headfirst, holding the shell upside down beneath it. *WUMP!* Morris's shell hit the pure snow as the creature holding him belly flopped atop him and came sledding down the hill, straight for Abbie and Jordan.

They leaped out of the way as a white-and-green blur whooshed past, plunging into a snowbank. Abbie and Jordan ran down toward the crash to hear the muffled squeal of Morris, laughing hysterically, trying to catch his breath.

"Again! Again!"

Two little clawed feet stuck out the exposed end of the shell as they reached him.

"Morris! Are you all right?"

153

Morris's smiling face poked out of the back of the shell-sled. "Hello, master! Meet my new friend, Wilford!" Abbie and Jordan stepped back as the snowbank seemed to come to life. A white-furred back stood and shook the snow off itself, spraying them with powder. Jordan and Abbie stood in awe, staring up at the Yeti.

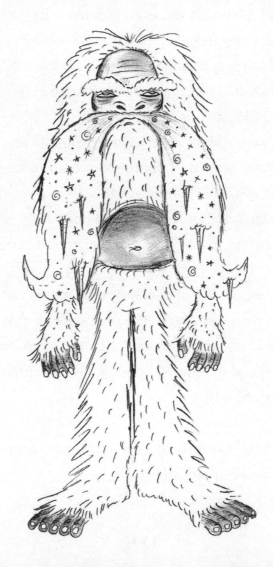

Wilford the Yeti looked most similar to Syd the Sasquatch, or Bernard the Skunk Ape. He was humanoid in form, and a biped, meaning he walked on two legs. He had apelike features: long arms and legs, and fur covering his entire body. But unlike Syd and Bernard, he wasn't a bulky or muscular creature. He was more thin and gangly, like an orangutan.

Most notably, however, was what hung beneath his nose. Wilford's thick, white, incredibly bushy mustache was encrusted with ice and snow. It sparkled with frost and twinkled with tiny icicles, and made him look a bit like he'd either fallen asleep with his head in a freezer, or had just won a plain-flavored snow-cone-eating contest. At the same time, it conveyed great age and wisdom. In fact, the Yeti reminded Jordan of an ancient but scrappy windswept tree—one better suited than a thick, massive redwood to survive the elements because it could willingly bend and bounce back.

Wilford studied Jordan and Abbie closely. There was a long silence until finally that great mustache rose as he opened his mouth to speak.

"Your friend here makes a righteous sled."

"Uh, thanks," Jordan said.

"Perfect for sliding all three of you back down off the top of my mountain." The Yeti turned and began to trudge back up toward his peak.

Abbie shot Wilford an angry glare, then knelt down next to Morris. "Are you all right? He didn't hurt you, did he?"

"No, master. It was fun!"

"What about your sara? How did you not spill?"

Morris bent his head toward her. "Look!" He tapped the top of his head. The water in his sara had frozen into a solid block of ice. "The cold turned my water to stone, so that I don't have to! I can now go with the flow, master! Anywhere I like!"

17

"Wait! Mr. Wilford, sir!"

The Yeti had made it halfway back up to the peak when he stopped and turned. He stared down at Jordan, still standing at the edge of the untouched snow.

"Please, no titles. It's just Wilford."

"Listen, we're not trespassers. The monks allowed us up."

Wilford contemplated this for a moment before answering. "No. The monks rang the bell. I allowed you up. And now, I'm allowing you to go back down."

Abbie joined her brother at the edge of the sacred snow. "We're not here as guests. We came as a favor. To warn you. There's someone searching for you."

"There is always someone searching for me," Wilford said. "And that someone is myself."

"Oh, brother." Abbie rolled her eyes. "Look. We're Creature Keepers. We're here to offer you protection. It's what we do."

"I am fully conscious of the Creature Keepers. And

I invented what they do." He turned to go again. "But none of this is my concern."

"Then you must know about Chupacabra," Jordan said.

Wilford stopped and turned back. "Chupacabra. There's a name I have not heard in a long time."

"He wants to steal your Blizzard-Bristles," Abbie said. "He thinks you're on Everest. We believe he's headed there now."

"Then it sounds like he is just as lost as he ever was. And again, not my concern."

Abbie was so growing so angry, she almost stepped forward onto the sacred snow. "I guess it's pretty easy to just sit on a mountaintop and not let anything be your concern."

"Actually, it's a lot harder than I make it look," Wilford said calmly.

Abbie continued. "What about the innocent people who live in the areas surrounding Everest? Are they your concern? Because when Chupacabra doesn't find what he's looking for, they'll be in danger!"

"She's right, sir," Jordan said. "Chupacabra has gotten more powerful. He's stolen Nessie's Hydro-Hide and one of Syd's Soil-Soles. He'll stop at nothing to get what he wants. And the next thing he wants is your Blizzard Bristles."

Wilford stared at the two of them for a moment. He looked past them, at Morris happily playing in the snow. "He seeks the power of the Perfect Storm."

"Yes!" Jordan exclaimed. "You've heard of it!"

Wilford stroked his thick, icy mustache. "He'll never get it. With my Blizzard-Bristles, I can summon ice crystals to show me what is happening anywhere in the world. I can send a single snowflake to the other end of the earth and land it on the wing of a ladybug—or just as easily blanket an entire continent in a hundred feet of powder. Chupacabra can seek all he wants. But he will never take my Blizzard-Bristles from me."

"Well, that's great for you and your 'stache-sicle," Abbie said. "But when he turns Everest upside down looking for them, a lot of innocent people will get hurt—or worse!"

"I use my elemental power to control all wind and weather on the planet. I do this to try and keep the world in balance as best I can. What people do within that world—that is not my concern."

"Fine." Abbie spun around and began heading back toward Morris. "Let's get out of here and let this frozen jerk keep searching for himself." Abbie yelled up to Wilford. "Maybe someday he'll find his heart."

Wilford turned and began trudging toward the peak. *Piff!* A snowball exploded against the back of his head. Jordan glared up him, angrily readying another snowball.

Wilford looked past Jordan at his grinning sister. "Wait, I'm confused," the Yeti said. "I thought she was the rude one."

"My sister isn't rude, she's right—you *are* a jerk! Our Grampa Grimsley was people, and you helped him!" He whipped a second snowball up at Wilford.

The Yeti ducked. "You two are descendants of George Grimsley?"

"You bet your blizzard butt," Jordan continued. "And he'd be disgusted to know you could've helped a bunch of people in Tibet who would be hurt by his archenemy but chose to do nothing! Now I get why they call you *abominable*."

"Okay, that was just hurtful," Wilford said. "You two wanna see something abominable? Follow me." The Yeti trudged down the hill, past Jordan and past Abbie. He walked to the edge of a cliff, where he scooped up a handful of powdery snow. As Jordan and Abbie approached, Wilford took a deep breath and blew the crystals into the air. Flakes whooshed through the sky in a trail of white, toward the west, like a river of diamonds. The ones that lingered sparkled and floated overhead. Colors and reflections began to form within the crystals. Suddenly, floating above them, was a moving image. It was a small, sunny village at the base of a mountain. A sign read: *Everest Adventures*. Crowds of mountain climbers were coming and going, gathering gear, eating, drinking, and getting ready to climb. They were noisy and messy; Jordan even thought he spotted a few of them littering.

"Look at them," Wilford said. "You see? These are the people you're asking me to protect. None of them is the human George Grimsley was. Your grandfather understood and respected the natural world. These men wish only to conquer it. For sport and for ego. What your grandfather accomplished was greater and more challenging than climbing any mountain peak. Rather than seek fortune or fame, he kept his greatest accomplishment secret from other men. For the good of the world. He was the opposite of these people. These people are the abominable ones. And they are *not my concern.*"

"Okay," Abbie said. "So maybe those humans are gross. And lame. And stupid. But they don't deserve to be hurt. When Chupacabra arrives there looking for you, whatever happens will happen because you let it happen—whether you consider it your concern or not."

She looked down at Morris. "Let's get you off this mountaintop. It's suddenly gotten a lot colder up here." Morris glanced up at Wilford, then dutifully followed his master.

Wilford looked down at Jordan. "I suppose you have something to say as well."

"Just that I think you're right," Jordan said. "My grandfather *was* better than those people. I know he was a great man who did great things, and not for fortune or fame. But I also know that if he were here, he'd do whatever he could to help them. And so will I." Jordan turned away from the Yeti and followed Abbie and Morris.

Piff! A snowball slammed into the back of Jordan's

head. The three of them spun around. Wilford stood staring out over the edge of the cliff. He took a deep breath, sucking in the freezing mountain air. He faced west and exhaled. The air passed through his giant mustache of Blizzard-Bristles and soared away into the sky in a blue, sparkling gust. Then he turned back to them. "Done," he said. "You can both stop making me feel horrible now. Okay?"

"Abominable," Abbie said. "Not horrible. What was that? Some Yeti-yoga deep-breathing exercise?"

"Look, a snowstorm!" Morris was pointing up to the sparkling powder image of the Everest village, still hanging in the air. Jordan and Abbie gathered to see. The scene was changing before their eyes, as the cold front Wilford had sent out arrived at the base camp eighty miles away. Wind began knocking over chairs and tables, blowing the coffee cups and litter around as the snow whipped in. The people bundled up and ran indoors to take shelter.

"Another way these people are unlike your grandfather," Wilford said. "They're such wimps. That storm will have them hunkering down in their goose-down comforters and indoor hot tubs for days. They'll be safe and sound and well out of Chupacabra's way."

"Okay," Abbie said. "I've gotta admit, that was pretty cool."

The Yeti smiled for the first time. "Cool? *That* was subzero, kid."

"Thank you," Jordan said. "But there are probably hundreds of base villages like that one at the foot of Everest. Even you can't just white them all out and hope no one steps outside. You don't know what Chupacabra is capable of now. Last we saw him was in the deserts of Xinjiang, and he nearly killed us. He needs to be stopped, once and for all."

"What else do you want me to do?"

"Come with us," Abbie said. "Help us stop him."

"No, no," Wilford said. "That's not possible. I don't leave my mountain. Not for you, certainly not for him, not for anyone. I'm sorry, but I'm afraid it's simply—"

"Yeah, yeah," Abbie said, walking off again. "It's not your concern. We got that."

Jordan gave Wilford one last long look, then sadly turned to follow his sister again. Wilford watched them, then felt two large eyes staring at him. He turned and looked.

"Well?" Wilford said to Morris. "Shouldn't you be off, too?"

"I wish to thank you. For playing with me before. That was fun."

"Uh, sure. Anytime."

"And thank you for sending George Grimsley to

play with me. That was fun, too."

Wilford was struck by this. So was Jordan, who stopped and turned around.

"What are you talking about," the Yeti said to the Kappa.

"Thousands of moons ago, my friend George Grimsley told me how it had been a great cryptid, high up on a mountain, who showed him the path that led him to me. I believe that was you. So, thank you." As he bowed, the ice in his sara didn't move.

"Morris, c'mon!" Abbie hollered. "You're not his concern!"

"You should probably go," Wilford said.

"As you wish. But if you happen to know of any other paths, please do let us know. We could really use one right now."

As he watched Morris trot off, he locked eyes with Jordan.

"Wait," the Yeti said. "There's something you should probably see before you go."

18

Abbie and Jordan left Morris playing contentedly in the snow and followed Wilford along a narrow ledge that hugged the side of the mountain. It was frosted with snow, and Jordan and Abbie chose each step very carefully—doing their best not to look down.

They slowly rounded the mountaintop until they reached the northern face of Mount Kanchenjunga. Here the ledge thankfully began to widen, opening up to a steep incline. Like the sacred patch they'd seen on the southern side, lying before them was a wide path of untouched snow, leading up to the mountain's peak. It sparkled and twinkled like nothing Abbie or Jordan had ever seen before.

Wilford led them both right up to the edge of the sparkling path and pointed. There before them in the otherwise perfect snow was a set of footprints, leading up the slope to the top of the mountain. And unless the Yeti wore a roughly size ten hiking boot, they were made by a human.

"Whose are those?" Abbie asked.

Jordan crouched down and touched the boot print. The inside of it wasn't soft, like the snow surrounding it. The print was solid ice. "It's Grampa Grimsley's, isn't it."

Wilford nodded. "The only human I've ever given access to the fifth treasure."

"But how are they still here after so many years?" Abbie asked.

Wilford answered by blowing gently on the tracks. A glistening sheen covered the boot prints, resealing them in sparkling blue ice.

Jordan stood up and looked into Wilford's eyes. "You preserved them."

Abbie smirked at the Yeti. "So for all your chilly-hearted, 'not my concern' abominableness, inside you're just a big ol' gooey marshmallow, aren't you?"

"Not at all. I just know how rare a pure heart can be. And I can recognize two more when I see them." Wilford stepped back and gestured toward the tracks.

Jordan and Abbie exchanged glances. "But we swore to the mountain monks we wouldn't step on the sacred snow," Jordan said. "I think we should keep our promise."

"And so you will. That is, if you can walk in your grandfather's footsteps."

Jordan looked down at the boot tracks, then up at the peak a few hundred feet above. Its shimmering snow sparkled in the sunlight. He carefully lifted his foot and placed it inside the first icy indentation. Then he did it again, taking another step.

Methodically placing one foot at a time inside their grandfather's ancient tracks, Jordan and Abbie treaded more cautiously than they had on the icy ridge. After a few minutes, they stepped out of the very last footprint—and onto the peak of Mount Kanchenjunga.

The two Elite Keepers stood there, frozen. Not from the snow that covered their shoes but from the breathtaking sight that was laid out before them.

"The five treasures of the high snow," Jordan said.

Extending out of billowing drifts of the whitest,

fluffiest snow they'd ever seen was a smooth, flat rock, jutting into the deep blue sky like a diving platform. Below it, Mount Kanchenjunga's northern face fell away toward the four smaller peaks. Beyond those, the great plains of Tibet and the flat deserts of Xinjiang stretched out forever.

"It's a lot more beautiful than gold or silver," Abbie said.

"And it's got grain and sacred texts beat by a mile." Wilford smiled.

As he stared out past the peaks, Jordan had a strange sensation of two opposite things being possible at the same time. The horizon seemed so far away, and yet, from where he was standing, he also felt like he could take one giant step and be on the other side of it.

"How can such a big world be so small?"

"I believe your grandfather asked a very similar question when I first brought him up here." Wilford reached out and scooped a pawful of fluffy snow. "It didn't make much sense to me then, either." He took a deep breath and blew, sending the twinkling crystals spilling out into the air, drifting toward the north.

"The snow up here seems so different," Abbie said.

"It's completely pure. Untouched by humans. It's been neither weighed down by footprints, nor dirtied up with fingerprints. I've done my best work with this stuff. You're too young to have lived through my big hits. The great snowstorm of the Maritime Alps back in 218 BC, that was a masterpiece. Then there was the New England nor'easter of 1978. That one was *wicked*, although between you and me it was a bit unplanned. I'd come down with the sniffles, and accidentally let out a whopper of a sneeze. It happens."

Wilford blew, more gently this time, on the crystals hovering overhead. As the light bounced between them, fuzzy images began to form, as before. He continued to gently blow, studying the images as if he were surfing television channels, then blowing again, scrambling the image and starting over. "Hm," he said. "Nothing."

"What are you looking for?" Jordan said.

"Not what. Who. Our friend Chupacabra. You said he was in the deserts to the north. I was hoping to locate him somewhere between the plains and the base of Everest. There's a lot to survey, but not much out there. I thought we might pick something up."

"Maybe he's gone underground again," Jordan said.

"Or maybe he's already there," Abbie added.

Wilford scooped two fresh pawfuls of snow and blasted them into the sky with his Blizzard-Bristles. A cloud of thick, sparkling dust headed due west. Soon the air directly overhead reflected back a wide, sparkling panorama of the majestic Mount Everest. Like a high-security camera feed scanning for intruders, the image consistently changed views and angles of the great mountain.

"I've sent out this surveillance storm to continually circle and contain Everest. It will send back any and all disturbances in the natural order of the mountain. It should do a pretty good job keeping people away, too. All we have to do now is wait and watch."

Jordan stared up at the images floating overhead. They were alive, constantly evolving and updating, swooping through the ridges and canyons of a mountain nearly a hundred miles away. The technical side of his brain was buzzing. "How does this work?"

"My Blizzard-Bristles allow me to do more than just blow snow and wind around. I can direct particles of precipitation out anywhere in the world. Their reflective properties interact with one another in an infinite number of ways. With practice, careful concentration, and very precise breathing techniques, I've learned to manipulate those interactions to bounce back reflections, creating a real-time image of what's happening."

"Kind of like what a satellite does with radio or sound waves," Jordan said.

"What I do is provide balance to light and matter. When balance is introduced to the basic elements of the universe, many things are revealed."

"So what happens when we spot him?" Abbie asked.

Wilford got a gleam in his eye. "That's when you get to see what these old whiskers can really do. I'll kick up the force of that storm a few hundred times and unleash it directly on our friend. He'll be pinned down in a tomb of ice so thick, he won't thaw out for years."

A soft, familiar ring suddenly echoed deep within Mount Kanchenjunga, gently reverberating through the cold night air surrounding the peak.

"Dinner bell," Wilford said. "It's been a very long time since I've had guests, but if you'd like, you may stay. Are you hungry?"

175

Both Jordan and Abbie smiled, suddenly realizing how famished they were.

"All right. Jordan, stay on Everest watch. We'll be right back. Abbie, let's go see what the monks have prepared for us. And let's all just hope it isn't tofu again."

Abbie and Wilford made their way back down and around to the southern face of the mountain. They found Morris sliding down a small hill on his shell. The three of them trudged to the edge of the wide-open shaft that led to the inner heart of the mountain. The bell rang out again, echoing upward from the darkness.

Wilford leaned over the edge. He took a deep breath and then exhaled gently through his bushy Blizzard-Bristles. An icy wind formed, exactly like the one that had lifted Jordan, Abbie, and Morris to the top of the mountain. It circled inside the shaft, spiraling downward. As it disappeared into the darkness, Abbie and Morris gathered around and peered into the abyss.

The howling wind echoed from below, growing louder as it began to whip back up the shaft. *WHOOSH!* The frosty gust shot out of the top, blowing Abbie's hair back. A large covered platter came floating atop the invisible spout of air and flew out of the hole. Wilford took a great leap and caught it, belly flopping into a snowbank. He sat up and smiled at the other two.

"Dinner is served," he said.

Wilford set out thick yak-fur blankets on the large flat rock for his dinner guests to sit on. Then he, Jordan, Abbie, and Morris gathered around the dinner platter. Laid out before them was a feast of rice, soup, fresh fish, and a bright-red paste spread atop delicious, fire-baked bread. "Mmm," Wilford said. "Banyan fruit jelly, and no tofu in sight. I should have visitors more often."

Everyone dug in, devouring everything on the platter. As they filled up on fish and rice, Jordan, Abbie, and Wilford kept an eye on the swirling, snowy surveillance image overhead. They warmed their bellies with hot soup and finally smacked their lips on the delicious banyan fruit jelly.

When they were finished, Morris sat back and stared up at the stars that were beginning to appear and twinkle in the darkening sky. Jordan and Abbie watched the ever-changing images of Everest flashing above them. There was still no sign of Chupacabra. They felt a happy fullness in their stomachs followed by a peaceful sleepiness steadily setting in.

Wilford spotted something among the dishes and leftover dinner plates. It was a folded note, with Jordan's and Abbie's names on it. He handed it to Jordan, who read it aloud.

> *Greetings, Elite Keepers!*
>
> *Hope all is well atop Mount Kanchenjunga. The monks and I are fine down here. I've been trying to contact Creature Keeper central command on the transmitter Jordan gave me, and after some trouble figuring out how to turn it on, I now find that I am quite unable to get reception. While I'm no technological expert, I suspect this may be because I am sitting beneath a mountain. Rest assured I will solve this challenge. In the meantime, be safe, enjoy your dinner, and I'll see you soon!*
>
> *Your friend,*
>
> *Eldon Pecone*
>
> *Badger Clan 74*

"I'll bet he could get reception up here," Jordan said. "Wilford, would it be possible to bring him up so he could join us? He'd really love this place."

"To the mountaintop, I suppose. But not this peak. This peak is sacred."

"Then why did you let us up here?" Abbie asked. "I mean, I for one wasn't very nice to you. Not that you didn't deserve it."

"As I said, I sense that the two of you are pure of heart." The Yeti paused. "Of course, the fact that you're George Grimsley's grandchildren doesn't hurt, either."

"Well, why'd you let *him* up, then?" Abbie asked. "What was so special about George Grimsley that you even kept his footprints frozen as a memento all these years?"

"Your grandfather was a young man when we met. He found me after getting a glimpse of the cryptid world and making a terrible mistake. He had seen with his human eyes a very special creature. And being human, he exploited what he saw, out of greed."

"But he changed," Abbie said. "He wanted to make things right."

"He was lost and wandering. I helped him by shining a light on his path. I showed him where he might find a way to make right what he'd done wrong."

Jordan sat up and pulled his grandfather's journal

out of his backpack. He flipped it open and read from it. *"This great creature has shown me my path and pointed me toward my destiny."* He looked up at Wilford, then glanced at the image of Everest shimmering above him. "That's it. That's what you did. With your snow-vision power to see anywhere in the world, you showed Grampa Grimsley where to find the cryptids!"

"I wondered how he located all those creatures all over the globe," Abbie said. "I can hardly ever find my iguana, Chunk. And he never leaves our apartment."

"Your grandfather took his first steps along his path down off this mountain. Then he followed it toward his life's work, helping many of my kind."

"It's because of you he became the very first Creature Keeper," Abbie said.

"Not just me. There was one other cryptid without whom your grandfather never would have started wandering in the first place. And now it seems that cryptid is trying to undo everything he unwittingly helped your grandfather create." Wilford stared off.

"Chupacabra thinks I'm my grandfather," Jordan said.

"I see some of him in you," Wilford said. "But I also see you're nothing like George Grimsley. I mean that in the best of ways. Unlike him, you are not afraid to ask questions. To truly learn. Your grandfather had to overcome his pride and his desire to conquer before he could open his mind and heart. I do not sense that conflict in you."

"Chupacabra said George Grimsley never asked the right questions," Jordan said. "That he never learned his history."

"It's true. Your grandfather was loyal, brave, and resourceful. He would set his mind to a task and get it done. But he wasn't very curious. He didn't look very far beyond what he considered to be his duty."

"Sounds like he would've made a perfect Badger Ranger," Abbie said.

"Chupacabra also predicted that bad things would repeat themselves," Jordan continued. "And we wouldn't recognize it until it was too late. What'd he mean? What questions didn't my grandfather ask?"

"Probably the same ones you're not asking me right now," Wilford said. "Maybe you are a little like him."

Jordan thought about this. Abbie saw her brother's confused expression and chuckled. "He wants us to ask him something, genius." She turned to Wilford. "Okay, I've got one. It's pretty basic. Where did cryptids come from?"

Wilford gazed past the Everest image, up at the stars. "Cryptids have been here for a very long time. But that does not mean we all came into being at the same instant, or from the same place. Each of the earliest cryptids was born with special, elemental powers. But even we were born at different periods of the earth's evolution."

"We?" Jordan stared at him.

Wilford nodded. "I was the first."

"How old *are* you?" Abbie asked.

"I was born hundreds of millions of years ago, out of a catastrophic event. A massive ice age that wiped out more than half the earth's living creatures at the time. As they were forced into extinction, I came into existence."

"And your elemental power is connected to snow and ice," Jordan said. "Coincidence?"

The Yeti shook his head. "That pattern repeated over the eons with extra special cryptids, each with its own unique elemental power. The second came with the evolutionary explosion of the first giant trees. Their roots stretched deep into the earth, deeper than any other plant before them. They were magnificent, but they affected the balance between soil and oxygen, wiping out even more species than my birth event. But from the rich, root-churned soil sprouted a new and noble cryptid endowed with Soil-Soles—which could manipulate the very earth they touched."

"Syd," Abbie said. "The Sasquatch."

"During the third great event, sea-level fluctuations

and other factors created the deadliest extinction the world had yet seen. It wiped out nearly every living thing but created a single magnificent one. She was born deep below the planet's newly changing waters— and given the elemental power to control them."

"Nessie and her Hydro-Hide," Jordan said. "And what about the fourth?"

"The fourth?" Wilford looked at him. "To my knowledge, there are only three of us."

"Chupacabra told me there was a fourth special creature with an elemental power," Jordan said. "One that even my grandfather didn't know about. Why would he make that up?"

"Chupacabra is a liar and a trickster," Wilford said. "But he is most dangerous because his reasons do not necessarily have to be rational."

Abbie looked down at Morris. His shell rose gently with his breath as he slept. "But is it possible?" she asked. "Could there be a fourth creature with an elemental power?"

"Anything is possible," Wilford said. "And I've been up on this mountaintop a long time. But I think I would've noticed another planetary catastrophe that gave birth to a fourth special cryptid."

"What about the others," Jordan asked. "The nonspecial creatures. Did they come from catastrophes, too?"

"Sort of," Wilford said. "We three elemental cryptids arrived long before the dinosaurs. We saw them come, and over the eons we saw them go. Their final extinction was brought on at the end of what you call the Mesozoic era. An asteroid six miles wide slammed into the earth, near what is now known as the Yucatan Peninsula. The mark of its impact is still there today. It sent tons of dust and vapor into the sky, blocking out the sun, eventually thrusting nearly three-quarters of all life into extinction, including the dinosaurs. But it also began a chain reaction of evolutionary anomalies that over time spawned all the various and unique cryptids you know. Plus a few you probably don't."

"Including Chupacabra," Jordan said.

"Chupacabra came up and made himself known to us around the same time the human race did. We three saw there was something different about humans, unlike any other creature we'd seen come and go on earth. They seemed harmless enough, but endowed with a unique ability to learn, and a survival instinct to control the world around them. Unfortunately, we noticed similar traits in Chupacabra. He wasn't like other cryptids. He was cunning and impatient, with a desire to rule over that which he had no right. He resented the powers we three had and believed we were wasting our gifts. He wanted us to act as gods. To control the earth and all its creatures. Including humans."

"Yep," Jordan said. "That's him, all right."

"We had no interest in Chupacabra's ideas of how the world should be."

"I'm guessing he didn't like that," Abbie said.

"It was a dark time. He lashed out at us, and then at less powerful cryptids."

"He killed his own kind?" Jordan asked.

"He was too smart for that. All cryptids instinctively know that if they kill another cryptid, their fate becomes the same as the one that they destroy. But he did cause harm, and pain—and panic."

"How awful," Abbie said.

"It was a cruel attempt to bait the three of us into joining him in ruling the world. But it didn't work. Nessie, Sasquatch, and I had witnessed too many destructive events that had wiped out so much life. We couldn't be a new force of misery to any living creature. But we had to do something to stop him. We set out to capture him, but he went into hiding. Even with my gift to see for miles, Nessie's ability to scan the seas and oceans, and Sasquatch's power to split the ground open to look under every stone, rock, and tree, we couldn't find or capture him. So we hid our cryptid brothers and sisters, scattering them all over the globe. Then we divided the earth into three sections, and each of us settled in a different area—Sasquatch in what are known as the Americas to the west, Nessie in the central European and African segment, and me here in the east. Together we vowed to use our elemental powers to keep the planet in balance, and to avoid another mass extinction—of cryptids, but also of humans."

Jordan thought about this for a moment. "We call ourselves Creature Keepers, but all this time, it's really been you guys who've protected us."

"You're People Keepers," Abbie said.

Wilford stared at the two of them, looking somewhat taken aback, as if reminded of something he'd long forgotten.

"Yes," the Yeti finally said. "I suppose we are."

As the night wore on at the top of Mount Kanchenjunga, the wind picked up and the temperature began to drop quickly. Wilford noticed his guests shivering in the cold as they watched the surveillance storm images of Mount Everest. Even Morris was trembling in his shell.

"There is no need for all of us to keep watch at the same time," Wilford said. He stood up and gently blew through his Blizzard-Bristles. A snow gust danced and swirled, whipping into a wide circle before them, forming a dome from the ground up. Seconds later, the last wisp of snow settled atop a perfect ice house.

"Cool," Abbie said. "It's kinda like a yurt."

"But frozen," Jordan added.

"A fro-yurt!" Morris exclaimed. He ran toward the

dome and dived, sliding feetfirst on his shell straight through its small entrance. Abbie and Jordan laughed as they followed behind. Before entering the fro-yurt, Jordan turned to watch as Wilford sat back down on the flat rock and continued to stare at the image of Mount Everest, all alone.

Inside the fro-yurt, Jordan found Morris and Abbie lying on their backs, staring up through a small, round hole at the top. The little igloo was surprisingly warm and cozy, and Abbie had packed snow atop Morris's ice-filled sara, just to be sure.

"Aren't the stars beautiful, master?" he asked her.

"Yes, and again, you don't have to call me that," Abbie said. "No one is your master. You're part of our team now. So just be your own Kappa. Got it?"

"As you wish, master. If you'd like me to get that, then it shall be gotten."

Abbie noticed a thoughtful expression on Jordan's face. "What's wrong?"

"Do you think he's lonely up here?" Jordan asked.

"I think he's grown not very fond of the rest of the world," she said. "I can totally relate—but yeah, I'd still get lonely up here, all alone."

"Being alone is not the same as being lonely," Morris said, continuing to stare up through the hole in the domed ceiling. "After a while, loneliness can become a companion. It just doesn't make very good company."

Jordan and Abbie looked at the Kappa. "You're a freaky little dude," Jordan said.

"Don't listen to him, Morris." Abbie lay down beside him. "So before Katsu and Shika became your Keepers, were you lonely?"

"Oh, yes, master," Morris said, still staring upward. "For thousands and thousands of starry nights I was all alone. At first it was good. Then it wasn't. And then it got much, much better. Once he found me. George Grimsley was very good company. I had such terrible trouble falling asleep all alone before he came along. He would lie with me by the riverside, and together we would stare up through the beech trees and count the stars until I drifted off."

"How long did he stay with you?" Jordan asked.

"Until the day he introduced me to my first masters."

"Katsu and Shika," Abbie said.

"And then I wasn't alone anymore, ever again."

"Morris," Jordan said, "after that, did you ever see my grandfather again?"

"Of course. I see him every night. I see him right now. Right . . . up . . . there. . . ." Jordan saw the stars reflected in Morris's big, beautiful eyes until they slowly closed, and the Kappa drifted off to sleep.

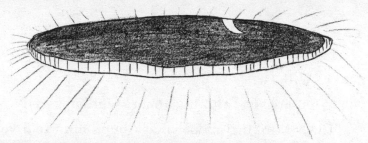

Abbie soon followed, leaving Jordan to stare through the hole in the fro-yurt. He thought about all the cryptids he'd met, and how most of them lived alone with their Keepers, hidden away from the world. For the first time, the thought of it made him sad. Each of these unique creatures had once shared a common acquaintance. The same first human friend. And that friend was gone forever. He thought about how alone his grandfather must have felt when he was wandering the world, until the day he met Wilford. Finally, he thought of Wilford, right outside, sitting all alone in the cold snow, staring at the shimmering image of a cold, lonely mountain eighty miles away.

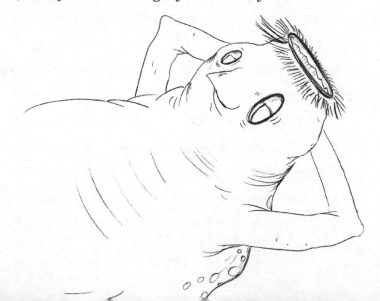

Jordan crawled out of the fro-yurt and sat down next to Wilford.

"What are you thinking about?" Jordan asked.

"I was thinking about what Chupacabra told you. About there being a fourth special cryptid born with an elemental power. Why wouldn't such a creature make itself known?"

"I don't know," Jordan said. "But why would three mass-extinction events create three special cryptids, then a fourth leave nothing but a mark?"

"That's a very good question."

"Here's one more," Jordan said. "It's about another one of Chupacabra's strange claims. He's always so sure I'm George Grimsley. It's like he can feel him, or smell him. I know he's a liar and a trickster. But I think he really believes it. And the crazy part of it is, in a small way, so do I. Sometimes I feel like my grandfather is still alive. Like he's with me, and he always has been."

Wilford reflected on this. "None of what you said was a question."

Jordan took a deep breath. "If my Grampa Grimsley was alive and you knew where he was—you'd tell me, wouldn't you?"

The Yeti pondered again. "Your grandfather had a path to follow. It led him to his destiny. And then, unfortunately, it led him into the mouth of a very large and hungry alligator. You also have a path, young Grimsley. And you must follow it to your destiny. There are no shortcuts, no glimpses into what lies ahead. There is only you, your path, and your footsteps. Anything beyond that . . . should not be your concern."

Jordan thought about this for a good long time. He was growing incredibly sleepy. It was cold, but he suddenly felt so weary that the thought of standing up and walking the few feet back to his warm blanket inside the fro-yurt seemed an impossible journey. Instead, he leaned against his new friend, his head resting on the Yeti's shoulder.

"Sorry," Jordan said dreamily. "But it's really cold, and you're really warm."

"Oh, uh—yes. Of course." Wilford looked down at him, and slowly extended a furry arm around Jordan. His gaze drifted back up to the image of Everest twinkling overhead, and he and pulled Jordan in closer.

Jordan smiled as he felt the warm fur surround him. "Oh, and Wilford," he said, drifting off to sleep. "None of what you said was an answer."

21

Jordan awoke to cold water tapping him on the forehead. He opened his eyes as he was struck with a ripe odor. As his eyes adjusted to the morning light, he peered through a greenish haze all around him and sat up. His head felt heavy, and a horrible grogginess overcame him. He stumbled to his feet and looked around. He was still on the flat rock, but everything seemed different. The billowing piles of pure snow were now nearly gone, melted down to a dirty green slush.

Jordan felt incredibly drowsy but fought to stay awake. The foggy haze, the smell—it all came flooding back to him. It was the odor of stinky feet. He looked up. The space overhead that had contained the sparkling image of Mount Everest and the trail of crystal powder that had delivered it was now a toxic, floating river of sludge sloshing above him, contaminating the entire mountaintop. All around him, what was left of the snow was vaporizing before his eyes into a green, toxic fog that filled the thin air. Jordan knew what this was. And who was responsible for it. They were being poisoned.

A panic set in as he looked around. Wilford was nowhere to be seen. And the fro-yurt had eroded away as if it had somehow rotted during the night. Through the haze, Jordan could make out a figure lying in the center of the remaining slush. He ran toward it.

"Abbie!" He leaped over what was left of the melting wall and stood in the center of the degraded igloo. Abbie was lying there, motionless. A chill rushed through Jordan as he lifted her and pulled her out. Morris was nowhere to be seen.

Fighting off his dizziness, Jordan carried Abbie away from the vile mist, over to where his grandfather's footprints had been. The entire slope down from the peak was melted away, including the preserved boot prints. He found a small patch of untainted snow and set her down.

"Abbie!" She was breathing but didn't stir. He shook her again, then scooped up some of the snow. He began to rub it on her face, not noticing the green river drifting closer overhead. As the poisonous drops began to hit the patch of snow below their feet, it burst into a thick vapor, overtaking Jordan's senses. He fell backward, rolling down the slushy slope.

Jordan lifted his head out of a snowbank. There was less green mist here below the peak, and he fought with all his might as his body and mind tried to shut down. He stumbled back toward the slope. He had to get back up to his sister. After struggling a few steps, he slipped and slid back down. Then he heard a horrible, snickering laugh.

Jordan forced his eyes to focus. He saw fresh tracks in a swath of untainted snow behind him. They were mismatched footprints, one clawed and the other much bigger and apelike. Even in his hazy state, Jordan knew those tracks could only belong to one creature. He stumbled as he followed the tracks, groggily making his way toward the laughter. He rounded a large rock and stopped short. There he gasped at what he saw.

"No! Get away from him!"

Chupacabra's head snapped around to look back at Jordan. He was looming over a furry white heap crouched against the rock. It was Wilford.

"Grimsley! How nice of you to join the party!"

Jordan struggled to stay conscious as Chupacabra stepped toward him. He held something behind his back with one of his claws. With the other he was carelessly tossing a small red stone in the air. Jordan tried to focus on reality, to hear what the creature was saying.

"You look tired, Georgie boy," Chupacabra whispered. "I told you, one way or another, you'd lead me right to what I wanted. And so you did."

Jordan strained to look past Chupacabra. All he could make out was a glimpse of Wilford's back. He didn't appear to be moving. Chupacabra stepped closer to Jordan, blocking what little view he had. "That stream of precipitation between Everest and this hideout served as a nice, clear path for me to follow," he said, flickering his scales menacingly, tossing the ruby-like stone in the air and catching it. "And once I dived into it, my Hydro-Hide basically did the rest, carrying me right to the Yeti's doorstep."

"No." Jordan struggled to speak. "Don't hurt him. He just wanted to be alone."

"Precisely!" Chupacabra cackled. "Which is why I have you to thank, for coaxing that abominable idiot out of his shell, and sending me such a clear signal! It would've taken me forever to find him up here!" He leaned in even closer to Jordan. "You really are becoming quite an asset, Georgie boy. I'm so glad I didn't get around to killing you."

"Don't hurt him . . ." Jordan's voice drifted off. Everything felt like it was closing in on him.

"Hurt my dear old friend? Now why would I do that? I just popped in to clean him up a bit! If he's going to reintroduce himself to the world, he needs to look presentable. So I gave him a little trim!"

Chupacabra grinned. Jordan's head began to spin. He heard the echoing laughter of the cackling creature. He was holding something up like a trophy. Jordan fought to keep his eyes open. He focused on what Chupacabra had in his other claw. Then he saw it.

It was Wilford's massive mustache, shorn clean off,

clutched in the horrible claws of Chupacabra. Jordan weakly reached out to try to grab the Blizzard-Bristles, but the cackling creature yanked it out of his reach. Jordan felt himself fall forward, his face hitting the cold snow.

Then everything went dark.

"Jordan, wake up! Jordan, can you hear me?"

Jordan's eyes shot open wide and he immediately felt a burning in his nostrils. The stringent odor was very different from the stinky-foot smell of the valerian root. Its effect couldn't have been more different, either—he felt like he was being shocked back to life. It made his eyes water and his entire face tingle.

Eldon held a small, broken twig under Jordan's nose—the same one he'd used to wake up Corky. "Oh, thank goodness!" He grinned, then yelled over his shoulder. "He's all right! Jordan's going to be all right!"

Zaya and Bernard rushed over and greeted Jordan.

"Whew!" Bernard said. "You had us worried!"

"So happy you're okay, Jordan." Zaya stood up. He began pumping a large tank strapped to his back. It was connected by a tube to a spray wand he held in his hand. He trudged off, pumping his tank and spraying an orange mist into the air.

Jordan sat up. "Where's Abbie?" Jordan said. "Is she okay?"

"She's okay," Bernard said. "But go easy. You guys have been conked out up here for a few days."

"What?" Jordan looked around. The entire mountaintop was a slushy, muddy mess, spotted with dirty green sludge-spots, which Zaya was busily spraying with his orange mist. The whole place looked like a war zone.

"Luckily, Zaya and Bernard were successful in finding that Siberian root and getting it back to the CKCC, where Katsu derived an antidote. They were in the process of synthesizing it on the sub when they got my distress call. That orange spray neutralizes the gas, in any of its forms. I'm just sorry that we got here too late to stop all this damage," Eldon said.

Jordan stumbled a bit but found his feet and stood. His head was clearing, and his vision was less blurry. He didn't like what he could see.

"Fresh snow will return to this place," Eldon said. "But I'm afraid the monks' underground canyons below were completely flooded. When the water came rushing in through the shaft you three came through to get up here, we knew something horrible had happened. But we didn't expect this. Somehow Chupacabra managed to gas this whole mountaintop with that awful valerian-root stuff."

"I saw it," Jordan said. "Up on the peak, when I first woke up. He created some sort of toxic sludge out of it. As it dripped onto the snow, it melted it and vaporized into that horrible, stinky gas."

"But how did he get it up here?" Eldon asked. "How did he even find you?"

Jordan thought for a moment. "The trail of crystal snow. It led all the way to Everest," Jordan said. "We used it to keep an eye out for Chupacabra. It was a ready-made river in the sky. A clever creature with a Hydro-Hide could manipulate it to carry him directly back to us."

"And deliver that valerian gunk along with him," Bernard added.

"But this wasn't Wilford's fault. He was just trying to help. He—" Jordan stopped cold. He looked around. "Where is he? Where's Wilford? Is he okay?"

Bernard and Eldon glanced at each other. Eldon nodded up the slope, toward the peak of the mountain. "You'd best go see for yourself."

Eldon ran up the slushy slope, remembering how his Grampa Grimsley's footprints had been washed away in the green goo. As he reached the top, he suddenly remembered something else—the last thing he saw before he blacked out. A panic gripped him as he looked out at the flat rock.

Wilford sat there in his cross-legged meditative position, facing the great horizon to the north. Jordan knelt down behind him and put his hand on Wilford's furry shoulder. He was hoping what he remembered might somehow be a nightmare, but he knew it had been all too real. "Wilford," he said gently.

The Yeti did not turn to face him. "It is not your fault, Jordan Grimsley. I should have known better than to get involved with matters that were not my concern."

"Please. Let me see."

Wilford turned his head. The great, bushy mustache had been shorn clean off. "It seems my Blizzard-Bristles have been stolen," he said calmly. "Quite literally right from under my nose."

Jordan was speechless for a moment. "Wilford, I'm so sorry. But do you know what this means? Chupacabra may have the power of the Perfect Storm! We have to find him and get back what he's stolen—from you, from Nessie, and from Syd!"

"There is another way," Wilford said. "To stay up here and hope that there is a fourth elemental power Chupacabra needs to complete the Perfect Storm—and that the creature who has it never makes it known."

"Wilford, that's not a plan," Jordan said. "That's just a hope."

The Yeti sighed heavily. "I know, young Grimsley. But it's all I have. And right now, it's the only thing keeping me from being hopeless."

"Listen to me," Jordan said. "I know things seem bad. But we can find Chupacabra, and we can stop him. We can get your Blizzard-Bristles back if we work together as a team."

The Yeti stared off into the northern sky. "I have nothing to offer a team. Please, young Grimsley. I wish to be left alone."

"But what if you're wrong. What if there are only three special cryptids, and he now has the power he needs to complete his plan. He could hurt millions of innocent people, and creatures, too! The world would be thrown out of balance forever."

Wilford faced Jordan. "Keeping the world in balance—*is no longer my concern.*"

Jordan felt his stomach drop. He stood up and stepped back. He stared at the Yeti. Then he heard his sister.

Abbie reached the top of the slope, her dark eye shadow running down her face. She was crying. Jordan left Wilford and rushed to her.

"Abbie," Jordan said. "I know. It's horrible. But at least we're all okay."

Abbie shook her head. "I've looked everywhere. Morris is gone."

"Chupacabra must have taken him," Jordan said. "But listen to me, Abbie. He won't kill him. He can't, and he knows it. Remember what Wilford said?" He looked over at Wilford, sitting with his back to them. "We're going to find him," Jordan continued, loud enough for the Yeti to hear. "And we're going to get Morris back safely. We're gonna take back everything that monster has stolen from us."

Eldon helped Jordan and Abbie onto the Heli-Jet, then signaled to Bernard and Zaya in the cockpit. As they lifted off the wet, slushy mountaintop, Jordan couldn't help but hope Wilford might suddenly come running toward them with a change of heart. As they circled over the northern peak of Mount Kanchenjunga, he peered down at the flat rock, hoping to see the Yeti waving for them to pick him up. But Wilford was gone.

They descended across to the four smaller peaks of Mount Kanchenjunga, then swung around and landed on a flat valley between the two lowest ranges, just a short climb above what was Banyan Canyon. The cargo door of the Heli-Jet slid open. Jordan, Abbie, and Zaya all gazed out upon a makeshift camp.

It was a horrible sight. The Kanchenjungan mountain monks who weren't injured were busily tending to the many who were. Some were setting up yak-hide yurts for shelter, others were kneeling beside their fellow monks lying on the ground, administering the orange antidote.

"Where are we?" Abbie asked. "What is all this?"

"C'mon, I'll show you," Eldon said.

Still others were pulling the last remaining water-logged monks up a long rope ladder that hung from a steep cliff.

They all walked to the edge of the cliff. More monks were climbing the steep rock, many with injured or unconscious brothers on their backs. Banyan Canyon was underwater, just as Eldon had described. All they could see now was a large lake. The series of slot canyons that once hid the underground home of the monks was completely flooded. Abbie stared vacantly at the last few soggy monks being pulled up to safety.

"Chupacabra's become a lot more dangerous," Eldon said. "Even without the power of the Perfect Storm, there's no telling what he might do next."

"Wilford didn't know anything about a fourth special cryptid," Jordan said.

"Well, if there is one out there somewhere, we'd better find it before he does."

"You mean *him*." Abbie spoke up from behind them. She wiped a tear away. "The fourth special creature is . . . him."

"Morris?" Jordan said. "Abbie, I know how special he is to you, but—"

"I just know it," she said. "Why else would Chupacabra kidnap him?"

"What would be his special power?" Eldon asked. "Turning to stone?" Abbie glared at him. "Oh. I'm sorry. I didn't mean that to sound mean, I just don't see how—"

She turned away and shuffled off toward the camp.

"She'll be okay," Jordan said. "Either way, we have to find Chupacabra, and fast. Any ideas?"

"The only thing I can think of is your GCPS system. Last we saw Syd's old collar, it was attached to Corky's tail. If that giant worm is still doing dirty work for Chupacabra, maybe we can get get a read on that collar and locate the both of them. Bernard's repairing the Heli-Jet now. He nearly burned it out trying to get up to rescue you guys. Once it's up and running, we should be able to access its onboard GCPS system."

"What about the mountain monks? Will they be all right?"

A gentle voice from behind answered his question: "We have survived worse," said the monk who was not named Jagger. "Not much worse, but worse."

* * *

Jordan, Abbie, Eldon, and Zaya spent the night helping feed and take care of the monks who were hurt in the flood, while Bernard repaired the Heli-Jet. The next morning, they loaded what supplies the Kanchenjungan mountain monks could spare onto the tuned-up Heli-Jet. Then the monks gathered around to see them off.

Jordan pulled Jagger aside. "Thank you for all that you've done for us."

"I extend the same sentiments to all of you."

"Us? But it's because of us the sacred snow at the peak of the five treasures was melted! Your home was destroyed, Wilford was stripped of his Blizzard-Bristles, and he's wandered off and will probably never trust another human being again."

"The universe works in cycles, young Grimsley. In time, the top of Mount Kanchenjunga will once again be replenished with snow, just as sure as the heart of the Yeti will be refilled with warmth. From what I have learned, it sounds as if you reawakened the Yeti's soul more than anyone since your grandfather. And so I am sure that Wilford, and the sacred snow, will return to us again. So yes, I thank you."

Jordan smiled. Then he thought of something. "Wait. What about the fact that we destroyed your home?"

"I will not lie, young Grimsley. That was a major bummer."

BRRRRR!

23

Bernard piloted the Heli-Jet south, toward the Bay of Bengal. As they circled the warm water where they'd crash-landed, he and everyone on board—Jordan, Abbie, Eldon, and Zaya—stared down in disbelief.

The entire Bay of Bengal was now completely frozen over. "Looks like Chupacabra's figured out how to use the Blizzard-Bristles he stole, too," Jordan said.

He and his friends circled over Sandwip Island, where the howler monkeys huddled together on the beach, their home covered in snow and ice.

Flying farther out, they saw the ice had spread far across the Indian Ocean. "Gosh," Eldon said. "Do you know how cold it has to be for an ocean to freeze like that?"

"There's no one out there," Abbie said, quietly scanning the frozen wasteland below. "Not a soul. I sure hope Nessie, Alistair, and Kriss are okay under all that ice."

"Is this the Perfect Storm Chupacabra wanted?" Eldon said. "Another ice age?"

"He wouldn't need all the other elemental powers to do this," Jordan said. "Just Wilford's Blizzard-Bristles. I'm afraid he might have something much bigger planned."

"What's bigger than freezing over half an ocean?" Zaya asked.

Frzzt! The cockpit radio suddenly crackled to life. "How about burying an entire continent under fifty feet of snow? Come in, Creature Keepers! Is that you?"

Jordan, Eldon, and Abbie leaped from their seats and crowded into the cockpit. Eldon grabbed the transmitter first. "Denmother Doris! Gosh, it's good to hear your voice!"

"Eldon! I've been trying to reach you for days! Are Abbie and Jordan okay?"

"We're okay," Jordan said, glancing at his sister. "But we've got a few cryptids who've gone missing."

"You don't know the half of it! We've got a monster

migration on our hands! Despite the massive blizzards hitting their areas, a bunch of 'em have gone AWOL again. I'm tracking 'em now!"

Jordan began fiddling with the Heli-Jet's GCPS as Abbie spoke into the transmitter. "Which ones, Doris? And where are they heading?"

"They're all from countries south of the Himalayas—East Africa, India, Thailand, Malaysia, even as far south as Christmas Island, and heading north as we speak. Alistair, Kriss, and Nessie were tracking them from below, until they got blocked in by the oceanic ice!"

"Oh, no," Abbie said. "Are they all right?"

"Don't you worry about that crew, dearie. They'll find their way out. Before I lost contact with them, Nessie was looking for a safe place to surface. They should have plenty enough air to last them 'til she does." This didn't make Abbie feel any better.

Eldon slid open the cargo door. A whoosh of cold air filled the cabin as he peered down at the snowy surface below. There was no sign of any submarine, and no sign of any wandering cryptids, either. Just snow-covered ice, as far as the eye could see. He yelled toward the cockpit. "Bernard! Try to get us lower, closer to the ice!"

"Yes, sir!" Bernard dived the Heli-Jet, then cut the jets and used the rotors to hover over the frosty Bay of Bengal.

Jordan had pulled up the GCPS and was studying the dots on the monitor grid. "I'm tracking them, but it looks like they've crossed the icy ocean and are already on the other side of the Himalayas, making their way north!"

"Look! There!" Zaya had joined Eldon at the door. He pointed at the ice below.

"Good work, Zaya!" Eldon yelled to the cockpit, "There's a set of tracks out here! A slithering groove in the snow! Looks to be serpentine. My best guess is it's Randy, the Sri Lankan Naga, and he's headed north!"

"Winner, winner, *chicken dinner*!" Doris's voice called back. "That big ol' snake is most definitely on the loose!"

"I'm locked in," Bernard said. He veered the Heli-Jet to following the snaky trail.

"Looks like he's crossed the mountain pass along with the others," Jordan said, consulting the onboard GCPS. "If we want to catch up with them, we're gonna need some speed."

"Buckle up, everybody!" Bernard hollered behind

him. Eldon and Zaya slid the door shut and scrambled into their seats. Bernard slammed the button marked Boost Thrusters. They zoomed over the frozen bay, heading north, straight for the narrow mountain pass above Bangladesh.

Even at boost-thruster speed, it was a few hours before they finally entered the corridor leading to the deserts on the northern side of the Himalayas. As they made it through, Bernard cut the thrusters and switched over to the normal jet engines. Everyone fell silent at the sight stretching out before them. As far as they could see, from the foothills of the Himalayas all the way up through Xinjiang, and farther north and east to the Gobi Desert, everything was covered in snow. A mean blizzard was just ahead of them, blasting the desert plains. And it wasn't letting up.

"Incredible," Eldon said. "The snow must be over a hundred feet deep down there."

Abbie noticed Zaya staring silently out the window. She felt the same dread that he did at the sight. "He's turned my desert into a frozen tundra," Zaya muttered softly.

FRZZZT! The Heli-Jet's radio transmitter crackled back to life, soon followed by Doris's shrill voice. "Come in, Creature Keepers! Denmother Doris again!"

"We read you, Doris," Bernard said. "And we're through. We see it." He swooped low, skimming over the flat, snow-covered plains. The wind whipped them around and the ride grew bumpy as they headed deeper into the storm. The only one not glued to the window was Jordan, who was still diligently studying the onboard Global Cryptid Positioning System screen.

"What about the runaway critters?" Doris said. "Do you have a visual on them?"

"That's a negative, Denmother," Bernard said. "We have no visuals on any creatures whatsoever! Are you sure you have your glasses on?"

"Don't sass me, Skunk-squatch! I know what I'm looking at!"

"She's right," Jordan said, pointing to dots scattered all over the GCPS map monitor. "They're down there. We should be right on top of 'em."

Doris confirmed from her end. "I'm tracking at least a good half-dozen cryptids!"

Eldon scanned the flat, barren, frozen terrain through his Badger Ranger binoculars. "Negative, Denmother. And we'd spot a muskrat dropping down there! Maybe the technology isn't working properly."

"Oh, hogwash, Eldon!" Doris's voice bellowed at him over the transmitter. "Jordan's technological installations work perfectly fi—" *KRZZZZT!*

"We lost transmission," Bernard said. "We've entered the snowstorm, and it's a real stinker. You all had better find a seat." The Heli-Jet shuddered, sending its passengers stumbling around the cabin and cockpit.

"Bernard, fly as low as you can without crashing!" Jordan was trying to get the GCPS to come back online. As the Heli-Jet swooped lower, it pitched violently, then steadied out a bit. The monitor in front of Jordan blinked to life. "Yes! If we stay close to the ground, we might be able to hold the transmission!"

"What good is that thing if the creatures aren't really down there?" Zaya said.

"It doesn't make sense that it'd pick up a signal if nothing were there." Jordan put his finger on one of the dots slowly moving along on his GCPS screen. "According to the system, that dot represents the Christmas Island Colossus Crab. She should be directly beneath us!" They gazed out the window as the Heli-Jet swayed in the crosswind.

"This is hopeless," Abbie said. "All that's down there is a blanket of snow!"

Jordan jolted up, as if he'd been nearly struck by lightning again. He looked out the side window, then at the monitor. Then he grinned at his sister. "Abbie! That's it!"

"What's it?"

"They *are* down there, exactly where the tracking system says they are—*they're just under a blanket of snow!*"

He turned to Eldon. "Chupacabra isn't trying to bring on another ice age. With Wilford's Blizzard-Bristles, he could have put the entire world into deep freeze by now. That's not his plan. He doesn't want to wipe everything off the planet, he wants to control it. He froze the Indian Ocean so cryptids could cross it! And he buried this desert in snow so they could travel to him undetected!"

"Of course," Eldon said.

Zaya peered out his window. "But how could they

possibly tunnel under all that snow?"

Jordan looked at Zaya. They all did. Zaya took in their stares. "Oh, right. Tunnels." A grin grew across his face. "Which means Corky's okay! I mean, still hypnotized and helping an evil, mutant creature, but aside from that, she's okay!"

"That's right," Eldon said. "She's just zonked out on that rare, Siberian valerian root."

"And I have the antidote now," Zaya said hopefully. "If we can find her, I can make her better, and then I can take her home!"

"Well, I can't land down there. I don't know how strong that snow is, especially if it's drilled full of wormholes. I'd feel awful if I accidentally crushed the Christmas Island Colossus Crab—she sends me a holiday card every year!"

"So what do we do?" Abbie asked. "Where are we going?"

Jordan looked back at the GCPS monitor. The creature dots were all slowly moving toward the same position. He hit a button on the console and a series of trajectory lines came up, showing the path each dot was headed along. They all converged on a single point. He hit another button and a digital topography map overlay appeared on the screen. Jordan pointed to the spot on the map where all the lines converged.

"Here," he said. "This is Chupacabra's big cryptid party. And we're gonna crash it."

"Okay," Abbie said. "But where's that?"

"Wait! I got this!" Eldon excitedly whipped out his beat-up, handy-dandy Badger Ranger pocket atlas. He studied the screen, then flipped through the worn pages. "Bingo! Got it!" He held up his map and pointed to a small name on the frayed atlas page.

Abbie peered at it. *"Medog, China."*

Jordan nodded. "Okay, then. I would never second-guess the official Badger Ranger pocket atlas." He leaned in closer to Bernard and muttered, "Especially when the GCPS mapping database confirms it. But let's not tell him that."

"That's it!" Eldon said proudly. "Bernard, next stop, Medog!"

24

Medog was a tiny, remote, and beautiful jungle area, nestled in a valley between the low hills of Tibet. It was usually thick with thousands of species of plants and trees. At least, when it wasn't covered in a hundred feet of snow.

As the Heli-Jet descended and approached from the west, the blizzard seemed to kick up and blow harder, toying with the chopper rotors, tossing its passengers around and blinding its shaggy, skunky pilot.

"Heads up, guys," Bernard said. "This isn't going to be one of my smoothest landings. And there's still a good chance we cave in one of those tunnels."

Jordan hopped in the copilot's chair. "We don't have a choice. It's not just Morris and Corky that are in danger." He studied the navigation system. "Okay, we're getting close. It should be just ahead."

"Not that we'll see it," Bernard said. "It's a total whiteout down there."

"What if we can't find it?" Abbie said. "Or if Chupacabra's gathering all the cryptids in some deep ice cavern somewhere?"

"Then we go and we get them," Zaya said. "If Corky's down there, I'll find her."

As they dropped lower, the wind pelted the front windshield with ice and snow so hard, Jordan thought it might crack. There was barely any visibility. The Skunk Ape leaned forward, his leathery snout fogging up the glass. "Wait! What's that?"

Jordan saw it, too. A tiny patch of green in the distance. He glanced down at the navigation system. They were right on course. "That's gotta be it! The center of Medog—aim for that, Bernard!"

WHAM! The Heli-Jet jerked as the wind slapped it. Bernard gripped the controls tightly, but they were suddenly spinning sideways. Jordan looked out the side window. The chopper was whipping so chaotically, he could no longer find the green patch.

"What's going on?" Abbie yelled. The passengers in back were all leaning from the momentum. "Are we crashing?"

"We're doing the opposite of crashing!" Bernard yelled. "We're caught in some kind of snowy cyclone!" Bernard yelled. "It's pushing us up, up, and away!"

Eldon yelled over the whining rotors and the howling wind. "Chupacabra's used the Blizzard-Bristles to swirl this snow twister, so no one can get anywhere near him!"

Jordan spotted the green patch pass by his window as they spun farther away from their destination. "Bernard! We have to hit the boost thrusters again!"

"You're crazy! What if we thrust straight into the snow?"

"Trust me! Hit the boosters!"

"Why is that your solution for everything?"

"Because it's our only chance! Now HIT IT!"

Bernard shut his eyes and slammed the Boost Thrusters button.

FWOOSH! The Heli-Jet jolted as the rocket engines kicked in. Bernard gripped the stick and did the best he could to point the Heli-Jet back downward, against the storm, toward the patch of green. They broke through the whirling wall of white, and he killed the engines and yanked the stick back, leveling them off.

KERRRASSSH! Everyone flew up in their seats as the Heli-Jet hit the thick snow and slid. Bernard employed all the landing gear in hopes that it would slow them down. The aircraft fishtailed in the snow and spun around wildly, finally sliding to a stop.

All was quiet for a moment. They could hear the blizzard howling overhead, but it was perfectly still where they landed. Jordan unbuckled his seat belt and ran to the cockpit window. Peeking out of the flat, snow-covered ground was a small sea of bright-green treetops. "We made it," he said. "Welcome to Medog."

Jordan, Abbie, Eldon, Bernard, and Zaya stepped out of the Heli-Jet and sank into the thick snow. With some difficulty, they trudged toward the nose of the aircraft. It hung over a steep, snowy slope that dropped about fifty feet to a lush, grassy floor. Beyond the grass was a circle of thick forest, dark and green like a jungle, and just as warm. It was a calm, tropical oasis in the center of a raging snowstorm.

"This is incredible," Abbie said. The thick tree line curved away from them on either side. "It's like a desert island or something."

"And I'm guessing the perfect spot for Chupacabra's little creature convention," Eldon said, consulting his pocket atlas. "Even without a swirling blizzard barrier to discourage any party crashers, Medog is one of the most remote places on earth."

"So where are the *invited* guests?" Zaya asked. "Where are the cryptids?"

Beneath their feet, the snow sloped away from them, the tall bank encircling the lush forest like a crater, forming a white fortress wall. Jordan slid down the slope and stepped onto the dry, green land. Then he turned around. "You guys might want to take a look at this," he said.

The others slid down and joined him. The hard-packed snow wall of the crater looked like Swiss cheese.

There were dozens of tunnel entrances. And they were all Mongolian Death Worm–sized.

Zaya looked at them. "You gotta give it to her. My Corky's a hard worker, especially when she's heavily drugged and under a deep spell."

"Chupacabra's valerian-root powder must have had that poor creature digging her lightning tail off," Eldon said. "She tunneled clear across China—a bunch of times!"

"We're going to free her," Jordan said. "*And* find Morris. *And* return all the cryptids safely to their homes. Oh, and we're going to stop Chupacabra, of course. And we're also gonna get back all the elemental powers he stole."

"When you say it in a list like that, it sure sounds like an awful lot," Bernard said.

"What is that?" Abbie asked. Deep within one of the tunnels, an eerie golden glow caught everyone's attention. It was getting brighter as it approached, like a headlight on a northbound train.

Eldon stepped forward. "If it's a cryptid, there's only one I know who glows like that." He held out his arms like he was going to greet an old friend. A very large old friend. He suddenly hollered down the tunnel. "Sandy the Sumatran Golden Liger! Get out here, you ol' pussycat!"

The Sumatran Golden Liger emerged from the tunnel. It was huge, with the body of an overgrown tiger, the mane of a lion, and the golden glow of the sun. Jordan had never seen anything so beautiful in all his life. And it walked right past the open arms of Eldon Pecone.

"Sandy?"

Abbie whispered to Eldon. "Dude, are you sure you're friends? Because he doesn't seem to know you."

"She," Eldon said over his shoulder as he watched the radiant creature head toward the forest line. "We go way back! Isn't that right, Sandy!"

"Sandy seems a bit distracted," Zaya said to Abbie.

Eldon's brow furrowed. He ran toward the Liger, who had stopped at the edge of the Medog forest to stare into the dark woods. "Sandy, what's wrong?" He got right in front of her and looked into her eyes. "Don't you recognize me?" Sandy stared back blankly and cocked her head like a confused dog. She sidestepped Eldon, then with great force pounced over the brush and disappeared into the forest.

Eldon turned around to face the others. "Did you see that? She and I used to be really close! I swear, you think you know a Liger, and then they just turn on you."

Jordan approached him. "Eldon, this is what Alistair described, when he said he found Sandy standing on the beach, remember?"

"Well, it doesn't make it any less rude."

"Zaya and I stocked the Heli-Jet with gallons of antidote to the valerian-root powder," Bernard said. "Why don't I go after her."

"I'll get my pump sprayer," Zaya said.

"No," Eldon said. "She wasn't poisoned. She showed none of the symptoms that Corky, Jordan, or Abbie did. This is different. Also, it's far too dangerous. You're not going anywhere."

Bernard shot Eldon a look. He looked like he was going to argue, but Abbie cut him off. "It sounds like we've got more company coming."

Suddenly, a half-dozen or so creatures of all shapes and sizes began stepping, crawling, stomping, and scurrying out of various tunnels. Like Sandy, they walked right past Eldon and the others, straight for the forest. They didn't look sleepy or brainwashed at all. If anything, they looked confused, as if they couldn't explain where or why they were wandering, but determined to get wherever it was they were headed.

"Ufiti! Srayuda! Francine!" Eldon ran up to them. "Stop! Where are you going?"

"It's like they're sleepwalking," Jordan said. "Like there's something calling to them." One by one, the creatures each disappeared into the jungle.

"What are we waiting for? We have to follow them!"

"Zaya's right," Abbie said. "I'm tired of waiting. I'm going in."

"Wait," Jordan said. "We don't know what we're up against. Chupacabra could have some new poison, or worse. If we just run in there, we could endanger not just ourselves, but all the cryptids who are getting sucked into his trap."

"What's he up to?" Bernard asked. "Why is he luring them all here?"

"He could be looking for the fourth special cryptid," Eldon said. "One with a special power that he needs to complete his collection."

"He already has him," Abbie spoke up. "And I'm going in there to get Morris back."

Before Jordan or Eldon could stop her, Abbie sprinted into the woods, following the path the cryptids had taken.

"Abbie!" She was gone. Jordan turned to Eldon. "We have to go after her!"

"Abbie's proven she can take care of herself," Eldon said. "Our priority is to protect those lost cryptids. And if one of them is the fourth special, it's imperative we get to him—or her—before Chupacabra does."

"*Psst!*"

They turned. Bernard was leaning his head into another tunnel. "I think there's another one coming! Let's ambush this one!"

Eldon stepped toward his cryptid. "Bernard, 'ambushing' is *not* proper Creature Keeper protocol."

Bernard rolled his eyes at his Keeper. "Well then, why don't you just welcome him with a big hug. It worked so well last time."

Eldon shot his creature a look, but Jordan stepped in. "We need answers, Eldon. It may not be by the book, but drastic times call for drastic measures. We'll gently pin down the creature long enough so you can do an exam with your first-aid kit, like you did with Corky. Maybe we can get an idea of what we're dealing with."

"Uh, pin it down?" Zaya asked with some concern.

"C'mon!" Bernard said. "It's getting closer!"

They all scurried up the snowy slope and perched over the top of the tunnel opening. The loud scrunching of feet in the snow grew closer.

"It sounds big. And like it has a million feet," Zaya whispered. "I'm really not good with creepy-crawly creatures. Maybe we should try to catch the next one."

"This from a guy who lives with a worm the size of a small train," Bernard said.

They all leaned over the mouth of the tunnel. The scrunching got louder. They leaned farther. Suddenly, just as the creature barely emerged, the snow gave way, and a mini-avalanche filled with three people and a Skunk Ape tumbled down on top of the large, unsuspecting cryptid, burying it in the snow.

There was a chaotic tangle of arms and legs and fur and snow as Jordan yelled to the others. "Hold him down!" The creature squirmed and kicked, flashing smooth tan domes mixed with different-colored fur in the melee.

"Ew!" Zaya yelled. "Its feet has giant humanlike toes!"

"It's like nothing I've ever seen before!" Eldon shouted.

"AAH!" Zaya suddenly squealed. "ITS TOES HAVE TINY FACES!"

Zaya had the toe in question caught in a headlock. It was staring up at him with a very annoyed expression. Finally, the toe had had enough and shouted back at him.

"WILL YOU PLEASE LET ME GO!"

They all froze. The polite-but-angry voice sounded all too familiar. Each of them climbed off. The toe emerged from the large clump of snow and brushed itself off, revealing itself to be not a toe at all, but rather the Kanchenjungan mountain monk who was not named Jagger. Four other toes followed suit, each shaking off the snow and revealing themselves to also be not toes. The mountain monks all joined in giving Jordan and the others very irritated glares.

"We're not used to the traditional customs of the outside world," Jagger said. "But this violent welcome seemed quite unwelcoming."

"That was my bad," Bernard said. "Sorry about that."

The large, white pile of snow suddenly shifted on the ground. The monks quickly scurried over to it and began to clear off the snow. A moment later they helped to its feet the great white creature who was lying beneath it. It was Wiford.

"You see?" the Yeti scowled at them all. "This kind of thing is precisely why I never leave my mountain."

25

Jordan rushed to the Yeti, but stopped short of giving him a hug. "What are you doing here? How did you find us?"

"The question is not how, but why." Wilford placed a paw on Jordan and took a deep, cleansing breath. "Since that last fateful day I saw you, young Grimsley, I have bravely undertaken a long, soul-searching, transformative journey."

"That day just a couple of days ago?" Jordan said.

The Yeti ignored him. "Those were dark times. My purpose on this planet had been quite literally stripped from me, leaving me with a deep feeling of emptiness—not to mention a very chilly upper lip."

Jagger and the other monks nodded sympathetically.

"I embarked upon a reflective wandering. A walk-about, to search for answers. I set out for the four remaining treasures of the high snow. How long my journey might take—that was not my concern."

"Couldn't have taken long," Jordan said. "It was literally, like, yesterday you left."

"As fate would have it, my very first stop brought me face-to-face—with *Destiny*."

"That's me," one of the monks said.

"That's *you*?" Zaya said.

The little monk shrugged and gestured toward Jagger. "I figured if he could just choose any name for himself, why not me? I've always liked *Destiny*. So that's my name now. Destiny."

Another monk piped up. "I'm *Quasar*! Cool, right?"

"I'm calling myself *Thunderbolt*," another said. "That or Ezra. Still on the fence."

Wilford cleared his throat. "Getting back to my story. It was Destiny who led me to witness an incredible sight. And reach a life-changing realization."

"I brought him back to camp," Destiny said. "I was having a pee in the woods."

"I stumbled out of the wilderness and came face-to-face with these giving souls who for years had cared for me. They were cold, hungry, and homeless. And here I was—lost, lonely, and bristle-less. Yet when they saw me . . . *they bowed before me.*"

The Kanchenjungan mountain monks were rapt in attention, grinning at the creature they loved. Wilford grinned right back. "It was at that moment, young Grimsley, that I knew I was just as lost as your grandfather was when he found me, all those years ago. And just like him, I realized I was never alone at all."

A warm chill ran through Jordan. He glanced at Eldon, who was wiping away a tear. The monks all went in for a group hug, embracing Wilford as he continued.

"I told your grandfather I was not concerned with the protection he offered me. I told myself I was all alone and didn't need anything watching over me. But I'd always been protected and always watched over. Not from above. From below."

He looked down. The mountain monks were still hugging him. A moment passed. "Okay. Thanks, guys. How about a little personal space? Still getting used to being around others, so . . ." They pulled away. "That's great. Thanks."

"Wait," Jordan said. "So you're saying you're here to help us?"

"Years ago, I set your grandfather on his path to give the cryptids hiding in this world the same safety, security, and peace of mind I thought I had on my mountaintop. I watched from that perch as he fulfilled his destiny. Now I understand it was humans all along who protected my solitude and provided my security." He smiled down at the monks, then looked grimly back at Jordan. "The protection you Creature Keepers provide to my fellow cryptids is under attack. Unfortunately for Chupacabra, this is now . . . very much my concern."

Eldon stepped forward. He lifted his hand to the brim of his hat, giving Wilford the Badger claw salute. "Welcome aboard."

"But how did you find us," Bernard asked. "And how'd you get here so fast?"

The monks scrambled over to the snow pile where Wilford had been buried and dug out a long, hand-carved banyan-tree toboggan. It had room for six mountain monks, and leather reins attached to a Yeti-sized harness.

"She can get moving pretty fast," Jagger said.

"Not as good a sled as that Kappa's shell, but still," Wilford said. "As for finding you, it wasn't too difficult. From the monks' base camp, we spotted many creatures heading through the mountain pass below. We sledded down the north slope, right into one of the tunnels. Then it was a straight shot all the way here."

"Excuse me," Zaya interjected. "By any chance did you happen to come across an enormous worm in your travels?" He spread his arms wide. "About yay long, maybe times a couple hundred or so, coos when you give her belly scritches?"

"Hard to miss," Wilford said. "She was snoring away in the middle of the tunnel. Looked yak-tired, the poor thing, but she wasn't injured. We squeezed around her and let her rest."

"She's okay!" Zaya ran to the mouth of the tunnel where Wilford had been ambushed. "CORKY! STAY STILL, GIRL. I'M COMING!" He scampered up the slope of the snow wall and disappeared inside the parked Heli-Jet.

"I'm so happy you're here," Jordan said. "And so proud you're joining us."

"Being part of a team is new to me, young Grimsley. But I'll do my best." He began strolling across the snow toward the jungle. "Wherever or however I'm needed, my sole purpose is to work with you all, as one. I totally get that now. Count me in." He turned toward the trees, but glanced back. "All right, then. I'll see you all later. I'm off to single-handedly get my Blizzard-Bristles back and kick that Chupacabra's butt. Shall we all meet up here later? Y'know, as a team?"

"What? Wait!" Jordan rushed toward him. "What are you talking about?"

"I'm going in. By myself. On behalf of the team."

"You don't do things *on behalf of the team*," Jordan said. "The team does things *as a team*. That's the whole point of being a team! We make a plan, and then figure out the best way to execute the plan, and then we— WILFORD!"

The Yeti nodded to Jordan, but kept inching his way closer to the forest. "No, no. This is good stuff. I'm listening. You keep explaining. I'll be back in a bit. But seriously, super teamwork!" He gave thumbs-up to the monks, who waved and applauded and gave thumbs-ups back. Jordan and Eldon turned to look. When they looked back, the Yeti was gone.

"Hey!" Jordan yelled.

Zaya suddenly came bounding back down the snowy slope, wearing his pump-and-sprayer tank. "Okay, I'm off!"

"Where are *you* going?" Eldon said.

"I'm going to save Corky. They passed her in that tunnel, so that's where I'm headed. I'm her Keeper, and she needs my help."

Eldon saluted him. "Can't argue with that."

Zaya saluted back, then trotted off in the opposite direction from Wilford, disappearing into the snow tunnel. Jordan couldn't help but feel things were falling apart. He looked at Eldon. "First Abbie, then Wilford, and now him? This is just great."

Bernard stepped up. "I'm still here. Skunk Ape Squadron, reporting for duty!"

"Oh, no," Eldon said. "You're to stay out of that jungle. You and the monks keep out of sight, and out of danger. Watch for any more cryptids coming through."

"But I want to help you guys," Bernard said.

"I know, but you can't. I need you out here. Try to get through to Doris, and see that the Heli-Jet is operational. We may need to make a quick exit."

Bernard stamped his foot, then turned to face Jagger and the other monks. "You heard Ranger Rulebook, guys. C'mon, let's go." He began hoisting them, one by one, up the snowy slope, so they could board the Heli-Jet.

"He and I are going to have a talk about his attitude when this is all over," Eldon said.

"Right," Jordan said. "But for now, we've got to figure out what's left to do." He looked down at his hand as he counted off all the solo missions that had suddenly split off. "Let's see, Abbie's gone to rescue Morris. Wilford's gone in to steal back his Blizzard-Bristles. Zaya's headed into the tunnel to save Corky. And Bernard is keeping the monks safe back in the Heli-Jet. Okay. So that leaves you and me to— HEY!" Jordan shouted at Eldon as the Badger Ranger suddenly leaped over the ground brush and ran straight into the dark forest.

"Don't worry, Jordan!" Eldon's fading voice shouted back. "I'll get to the bottom of whatever's mind-controlling those cryptids!"

Jordan stood near the edge of the jungle, one foot on the green grass, the other in the snow. "Okay, then," he said as he stepped into the jungle. "I guess that leaves me to just take care of trying to find the cryptid with the mysterious fourth elemental power who may or may not exist." He suddenly shouted out to nobody: "Great job, everyone!"

The thick forest was humid and teeming with life, especially compared to the cold and barren expanse surrounding it. There were exotic plants and flowers Jordan had never seen before, bursting with color from the moist, rich soil beneath his feet.

He made his way in the direction Wilford had disappeared, dodging the bamboo and leaping over the wild mushrooms and massive ferns, trying his best to employ Eldon's spooring techniques. He noticed a small patch of white fur hanging from a low branch not too far in front of him. Against the rich, bright colors of the lush forest, this tuft of white stood out like a mini-marshmallow atop a spinach salad. He stopped and inspected it, then studied the trees nearby. Up ahead, he eyed another tuft of white.

He collected more and more tufts of white fluff as he reached the top of a long, sloping hill. There was a clearing ahead, and Jordan quickly ducked behind a large bush. A tall man on a stone table with his back to Jordan sat staring at a large, vine-covered stone wall in front of him. The ground around and under the man was littered with the same white fluff Jordan had been plucking as he spoored his way toward Wilford. Unless Chupacabra decided to shave the *rest* of Wilford, all this white fluff wasn't adding up.

The man sitting near Jordan had slick black hair and wore a long trench coat. He was very tall, with legs that dangled from the stone table. A cold chill dropped into Jordan's stomach as he suddenly recognized him. It was Señor Areck Gusto.

It couldn't be, Jordan thought. There was no reason Jordan could think of for Chupacabra to disguise himself again. Besides, in order to transform, the cryptid would need to find and use a sacred half human, half cryptid, called a *cryptosapien*, and those were not only very rare, but in Jordan's experience they were also very stubborn and annoying. But there was Gusto, Jordan was sure of it. The other thing he was sure of was that disguised or not, if this was Chupacabra, Jordan had to make a move.

He steadied himself for a surprise attack, calming his nerves with the observation that Gusto appeared to be missing all three of the powers that Chupacabra had stolen. Along with the element of surprise, this gave Jordan the confidence he needed to single-handedly try and overtake Chupacabra. It was now or never.

Jordan moved out of his hiding spot, readying himself for an attack, when a voice suddenly stopped him cold, forcing him to duck behind the brush again.

"Well, there you are! Sitting right where I left you, hee-hee . . ." The voice was high-pitched and raspy, an old man's voice. Jordan had heard it before. It belonged to someone he never expected to see again.

A wrinkly old man stepped out in front of Gusto, looking just as bald and hunched as he did the last time Jordan had seen him, the night Jordan thought he had drowned. "Harvey Quisling?" Jordan whispered to himself.

Harvey was an ex–Creature Keeper, one who had betrayed the rest of them. He'd been the Keeper of Peggy, the Giant Desert Jackalope, but had abandoned his cryptid to help Gusto kidnap the Loch Ness Monster. Once Gusto had no more use for Harvey, he cast the old man aside. But apparently, the foolish traitor was back.

"You're looking good, Señor Gusto." The old man

snickered. "Thanks to me, as usual, hee."

Gusto didn't budge, even as Harvey leaned in very close to him. "What's that?" He held a hand to his ear. "What did you say? You're sorry for everything you did to me? Is that right? Well guess what, Señor?"

WUMP! Harvey suddenly punched Gusto in the belly. "Apology denied!" A tuft of white fur flew up as Harvey laughed in Gusto's face.

Jordan looked down at the white fur in his hand. It was the same stuff.

"QUISLING!" The little old man spun around at the sound of this new voice. It made the hair stand up on the back of Jordan's neck.

"Y-yes, Chupacabra!" Harvey began picking up the pieces of white fluff and frantically stuffing them back into Gusto's jacket. "Coming, sir!" He shuffled off, around to the other side of the vine-covered, ancient-looking stone wall, leaving Gusto sitting perfectly still.

Jordan slowly crept out from behind his bush again. If this man wasn't Chupacabra in disguise, then who was he? As Jordan approached, the seated figure began to slowly slump over. *Maybe he's conked out on that Siberian valerian root*, Jordan thought. *This should be easy.*

Jordan leaped, tackling Gusto off the table and onto

the floor. He pinned him down and looked at who—or rather, what—he was fighting.

It was a fake Gusto. Not that Gusto hadn't always been a fake, but this wasn't a fake in the sense that it was a disguise for Chupacabra. This was a *fake* fake—a life-sized doll, stuffed with white fluff, sewn together, and dressed in Gusto's clothes. The greasy black hair was just waxy yarn sewn to a pillowcase, with a rather crude likeness of Gusto's eyes, nose, and mouth stitched onto it. Jordan picked up the doll and stared at the pillowcase face.

"No wonder Harvey Quisling was so brave with you," he said. He placed the doll back on the table, then looked over at the stone wall where Harvey had disappeared. He carefully approached it and peered around to the other side. He was apparently in the backstage section of an ancient amphitheater. On the opposite side of the wall was the stone stage, and before it was a grassy clearing. Assembled in that field, silently staring blankly up at nothing, were dozens of cryptids of all shapes and sizes. But none of them looked particularly special.

"He's got them all hypnotized," Jordan said to himself.

"Look at them, Quisling!" Chupacabra's voice was just a few feet from Jordan's head, right on the other side of the wall. He ducked back and listened the best he could.

"Assembled out there is our future army," Chupacabra's voice continued. "The Cryptovian Homing Utility Persuading Apparatus we attached to that collar has worked even better than I planned."

"Y-yes, sir," Harvey stammered. "Moving it here attracted so many more cryptids than the test we conducted in the middle of the desert."

"And it works because of those tracking collars the Creature Keepers so helpfully gave all the cryptids! We must remember to send them a thank-you note for providing such reliable technology!"

"Yes, yes." Harvey giggled. "Hee-hee—"

"Shut up, Quisling. Have you prepared the puppet?"

"Of course, sir. Some of my best needlework, if I do say so—"

"Well, it had better work, or you'll find yourself exiled again. And next time, I won't take you back."

"Sir, why not just use their tracker devices to force them to follow you?"

"Because you can lead a creature to war, but you can't make him fight. The signal from my apparatus to those collars only lured them here. I have to win their *hearts*, Quisling. Just as I've won yours."

"And what if you can't?"

"Well, that will be unfortunate—for them. I'd prefer my army follow me of their own free will. If not, I have enough valerian-root powder to put them all to sleep for a long, long time."

"I'm sure they will accept you as their true leader—especially once you trick them with your hoax of beating up a giant doll!"

There was a moment of silence. "Shut up, Quisling."

"Right. Of course. Sorry, sir."

"This had better go perfectly. I need my cryptid army to begin preparing for Operation Pangaea while I firefly to collect the fourth elemental power necessary to create the power of the Perfect Storm!"

"Um, forgive me, sir, but fireflying that distance will require using up your very last blaststone."

"Don't tell me that, Harvey. One stone was all I needed to firefly back and forth between Canada and the Amazon."

"Yes, but that was half the distance, sir. And you've already depleted this last stone to reach the Himalayas, and then to melt the Yeti's trail, and I fear that—"

"SILENCE, QUISLING!" Jordan jolted at Chupacabra's hot anger. "The only thing you should fear is your personal extinction. Because that will be my sole focus on this earth if I fail to reach that fourth elemental power."

"I will not let you down, Chupacabra, sir."

"I hope not, Quisling. It would be tiresome to have to kill you twice. Now go!"

Jordan dived back behind the brush to hide again just before Quisling returned around the wall to the backstage area. It was all Jordan could do to contain his rage at hearing how his tracking devices—the very pieces of technology he'd created to protect the creatures—were being used to lure them to danger.

Harvey looked even paler, his bald head beaded with sweat. He buttoned up the jacket of the life-sized Gusto puppet and attached it to some wires that were hanging down from the rafters. He smacked the puppet in the face. "I hope you were listening," he snarled at the doll as he hobbled off. "Do not blow this for us."

Quisling then exited along the back wall, disappearing around the far corner.

Jordan's mind was racing as he tried to think of what to do next. He needed to get the collars off all the cryptids and wake them up. He also needed to find Abbie and see that she and Morris were all right. Finally, Eldon needed to know all that he'd just overheard. Chupacabra didn't have the power of the Perfect Storm, and the last mystery special cryptid wasn't among the ones gathered in Medog. Still, Chupacabra was more dangerous than ever. "First, I'd better find that Yeti before he kills himself," he mumbled aloud.

He turned to run and slammed into a white, furry wall. Wilford was standing directly behind him. "Seek and ye shall find," the Yeti said as he helped Jordan up off the ground. "Now if you'll excuse me, I have to see a thief about my Blizzard-Bristles."

"Wilford, you can't," Jordan said. "Not now. Chupacabra has too much power. He won't think twice about hurting you."

"My own personal safety is not my concern."

"Okay, then let me show you something else." Jordan pulled the Yeti by his paw, out past the Gusto puppet and up to the wall. He peered around it as before, showing Wilford what was on the other side. Wilford's expression changed as he stared out at the dazed cryptids in the audience.

"What about them?" Jordan whispered. "Are you concerned about *them*? Listen, I know you want to take on this fight all by yourself, to make things right without anyone else's help. I used to think that way, too. But I learned how to be part of something bigger than myself. I learned it's the best way. And trust me— against Chupacabra, I've learned it's the only way." He nodded toward the cryptids. "Look at them. A long time ago you chose to protect them, and you trusted a Grimsley to help you do it. I'm just asking you to trust a Grimsley again."

Wilford looked down at Jordan. A smile crept over his bare lip.

Jordan smiled back. "Okay," he said. "Now tell me, what do you know about hoaxing?"

The audience of dazed cryptids reminded Abbie of the reaction she got when she read her ten-page gothic poem, *Scaly and Cold: An Ode to Chunk,* to her class.

She moved quickly around, behind, and beneath them, keeping her head low as she searched for Morris. There were reptilian cryptids, creatures that resembled giant bugs, ones that were little more than massive gobs of goo, and more than a few hairy, apelike animals. But none were her turtle friend.

"Morris!" she whispered. "Morris, where are you?" She stepped over a large, creepy-crawly Vietnamese cryptid who happened to be named Conrad. He sported hundreds of tiny, millipede-like legs, and under normal circumstances was very curious by nature. But he barely registered her as he continued to stare straight ahead.

A strange growl from across the field caught her attention. Eldon was forcing a physical examination on an irritated-looking dragon-like creature with scaly skin and a saber-toothed tiger's head. She ran to him, keeping her head down.

"Seriously, Paul?" Eldon said. "You're going to growl at me now? Remember when I gave you that emergency root canal a few years back? You barely made a peep. Now open up and let me look at your tongue or I'm going to lose my temper!"

"Eldon!" Abbie said. "Are you insane? What are you doing?"

"Hello, Abbie. I'm just trying to figure out what's gotten into these creatures. They're perfectly lucid, they just seem to be focused on something they can't see. And if Paul here would simply *cooperate*, I could check his tongue for any toxins. But instead, he's being a *big baby*! AREN'T YOU, PAUL?"

"You picked him to start with? That thing could rip you in half!"

"Paul is an African Dingonek. Jungle Walrus. And frankly, I'd like to see him try. He'll find out in a jiffy just how fast I can report his scaly butt to his Keeper, who I'm sure is already displeased that he's gone missing." Eldon pushed the tongue depressor toward the cryptid's mouth and tried to cram it in. The beast kept its huge jowls sealed.

"Okay, mister!" Eldon said, pointing his tongue depressor menacingly at the beast. "You are on notice! I am *very* disappointed in you!" Abbie dragged Eldon away from the Dingonek.

"Eldon, you've got to help me. I can't find Morris anywhere. He's not in the crowd. I'm starting to fear the worst. The water in his bowl must have melted by now. If he spills and turns to stone just one more time, we can't change him back!"

"I wasn't sure I should tell you this," Eldon said. "But the first quarter moon rises again tonight, at midnight. Once it does, Morris's cycle resets. We just have to keep his head from spilling until then. Don't worry. We'll find him."

Jordan came running up to them, excited and out of breath. "I know what's happened to the cryptids! It's the GCPS bracelets! Chupacabra attached some sort of homing device to Syd's nasty old tracker! He's essentially hacked our tracking system, and is sending an impulse that's led them all here. That old collar has been regurgitated, pooped out, and dragged underground on the tail of a Mongolian Death Worm—and now it's here somewhere, luring those cryptids to it! We've got to get the bracelets off these creatures!"

"Where's Wilford?" Eldon said.

"Wilford's here?" Abbie said.

"He's backstage," said Jordan.

"There's a backstage?" Eldon said.

"Jordan, please tell me you saw Morris back there."

"No, I didn't. But Abbie, there's something you should know. Morris isn't the special cryptid. I mean, he's special. He just doesn't have the fourth elemental power. I overheard Chupacabra. Whatever this mystery cryptid is, both it and its special gift are thousands of miles from here."

"I guess you were right," she said to Eldon. "Turning to stone isn't a special power. Just a curse."

"Don't say that," Eldon said. "We still have to find him. And we will."

"No," she said. "*I* will. It was my job to keep Morris safe. And that's what I'm going to do, especially now. If Chupacabra has no need for him, he's in more danger than we thought." She turned toward the stage and made off through the crowd of cryptids.

"So, what's Chupacabra up to?" Eldon asked. "Why are all these cryptids gathered here if he isn't looking for the fourth special creature?"

"He's wants to form an army," Jordan said. "He's gonna try to get them to join him."

"And how in the world does he think he can do that?"

"He's planning a hoax."

"A *hoax*? So what's our plan?"

"We're Creature Keepers. We'll out-hoax him. But first we need to get those tracker devices off these cryptids. We need them thinking straight."

"Okay," Eldon said. "Just don't start with Paul. He's in a mood."

They turned to the nearest cryptids and located their tracking devices. But getting them off wasn't as easy as they hoped it would be, especially when the creatures refused to cooperate. Before they could remove a single collar, in fact, the entire gathering of cryptids had begun shuffling toward the stage, packing in tightly, like it was feeding time at the crypto-zoo. Caught up in the moving cluster of scales, fur, spikes, and leathery hides, Jordan and Eldon had to dance to avoid being trampled. When they found themselves near the back of the crowd, they stood up and faced the stage to see what all the commotion was about.

Chupacabra stepped out of the wings of the

amphitheater and stood at the center of the stone stage. He peered out at the unblinking stares of his fellow cryptids. His giant club foot of a Soil-Sole was still melded to his left leg, and his skin was still a suit of shimmery scales, thanks to the hijacked Hydro-Hide. And around his neck was Syd's old GCPS tracker collar, complete with the Cryptovian Homing Utility Persuading Apparatus attached to it.

"Greetings, and welcome, my brothers and sisters!" Chupacabra bellowed to the rapt audience. Every cryptid eye was glued to the collar around his neck. "Welcome to your first day of freedom! Freedom from hiding! Freedom from fear! Freedom from man! And especially, freedom from . . . THE CREATURE KEEPERS!"

The cryptids continued to silently stare at Chupacabra. "My, what an attentive crowd you are. Oh! Of course. You're still shackled with the leashes of your human overlords. As am I—behold!" Chupacabra pulled Syd's collar off his neck and held it high. All the heads in the audience followed it like a pack of golden retrievers staring at a tennis ball.

Chupacabra dropped the CHUPA-enhanced collar on the stage. All eyes followed as he lifted his great Soil-Sole over the device.

"My friends, welcome to the next stage in your crypto-evolution. And the first stage in your crypto-*revolution*."

CRUNCH!

With one step of his Soil-Sole, Chupacabra crushed Syd's tracking bracelet.

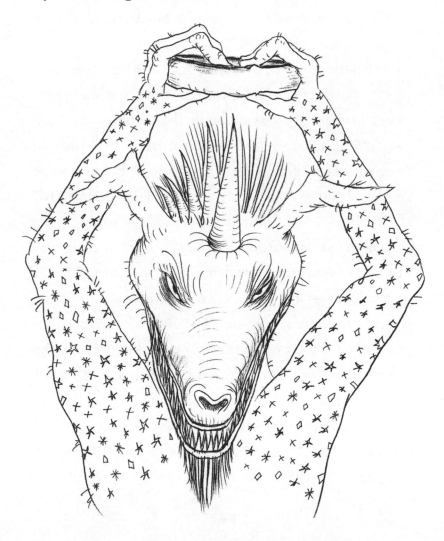

HEH
HEH
HEH

28

Abbie snuck her way along the crumbling, mazelike stone walls that made up the backstage of the ancient amphitheater. As she searched for Morris, she could hear a commotion coming from the stage. She hoped no one was in danger. But her sole focus was to locate Morris and get him to safety.

She turned a corner and stopped short at an odd sight. A hunched, bald little old man stood atop a large stone. He seemed to be preparing some sort of soup inside a much larger crate. "Time to make the medicine, hee-hee," he said to himself. He held his nose as he poured a large amount of green powder from a sack into the top of the crate. Abbie couldn't see clearly what it was, but she could smell it. The odor of stinky feet—valerian-root powder.

She crept closer as the little old man tossed the empty sack aside and began stirring whatever it was he was making with a mixing stick. He stopped and turned, listening intently. Abbie froze in her tracks. Chupacabra's voice echoed from out on the stage. The little old man quickly finished stirring, and Abbie ducked behind the wall. He then hopped off the stone and ran past her, mumbling to himself. "Must be ready with the puppet! Almost showtime, hee-hee!"

Abbie watched the strange old man run to a rope ladder hanging from the tree-branch rafters running out over the main stage. As he climbed, and once the coast was clear, she approached the noxious stew he'd been preparing. As she came around the side of the large crate, her heart suddenly sank. It was a cage. The front of it was barred, and through those bars, with just enough room to stand captive, was Morris.

The turtle cryptid's eyelids were drooping, but he was alive. "Thank goodness! Can you hear me, Morris?" She stepped onto the large stone and looked at the top of the crate-cage. There was a hole cut in it, the same diameter as Morris's sara. A chill came over her as she looked down through it. She was relieved to see that Morris's sara was filled, but alarmed at the color. The water inside was a vile green color. She looked to the floor. The empty sack was still lying beside the cage.

"Oh, no," she said through tears. "What have they done to you?"

The sound of her voice seemed to pull the creature out of his daze. His eyes focused slightly on her face, and he mustered a small smile. "Hello, master . . ."

Abbie was relieved to hear his voice, as weak and raspy as it was. "Morris, listen to me carefully. You've got something bad in your sara, and it's seeping into your head, making you sleepy. I'm going to get you out of here, but it's important that you stay awake, do you hear me?"

"As you wish . . . master. . . ." His voice trailed off as his eyes glazed over again.

"Morris, no! Wake up!" Abbie shook the cage, jarring her friend and sloshing the green water around in his deep head bowl. Abbie stopped immediately as she realized the impossibility of her situation. She had to get that poison out of his sara before it knocked him out, but she couldn't empty it or he'd turn to stone permanently. She unlatched the cage, and the door swung open. As she carefully led him out, his head drooped drowsily.

"Morris! Wake up!" She held his head steady so as not to spill. "MORRIS!"

The cryptid shuddered and woke again, his eyes

slightly more focused as he saw her. He smiled a little. "Master . . . it is so good to see you. . . ."

"You too. Now we're going for a walk together, you and I. We're going to find some clean water, and replace the bad water in your head, do you understand?"

"As you wish, master."

She put her arm around his shell and led him slowly behind the wall. "We're gonna be okay, Morris," she said. "I'm just glad you're alive. Now let's stay quiet. *And awake.*"

29

As the cryptids came out of their collective trance, they looked around the amphitheater field where they were gathered. Many seemed nervous. Others looked suddenly quite uncomfortable. Every one of them was, at the least, rightly confused.

"Yes, yes, take it all in!" Chupacabra grinned as he stared out at them. "Even your fear! Look around you. There are no Creature Keepers here! But do not distress. Freedom can be frightening at first!"

Anxious squeals and grunts rose from speaking and nonspeaking cryptids alike. One who did have the power of speech, the elf-like Indonesian Ebu Gogo known as Eddie, shouted up toward the stage.

"Where are they?" Eddie asked. "Where are our Keepers?"

"They are in the past, where you left them—in the dark caves and dank burrows where they hid you from the world! But today begins your future. You are all completely on your own! You are free cryptids!"

A cacophony of growls and squeals and howls and hisses rose up from the crowd. Some of the creatures shuffled and backed away from the stage, while others looked around and soaked in this new experience.

Barry, a bloated salamander-type cryptid known as a Himalayan Buru, reared up on his two hind legs. "We *know* we're cryptids. But what the heck are you?" Barry wasn't one to beat around the bush.

Chupacabra spoke loudly, so that the very last creature in the very back of the outdoor amphitheater could hear him. "You all know me! You've heard the myths and you've been fed the lies for years! I'm the cryptid your creature captors couldn't keep. The one they feared, then taught you to fear. But you must forget their lies. I am not your enemy, nor your captor! I am just like you—a cryptid in its natural state, free to roam the world, under no one's control but its own! Any of you may leave right now if you like. But before you do, consider this—I am the one who freed you. I am the one who safely brought you together! And I am

the one who now calls on you to join forces with me—
Chupacabra!"

Francine, a swamp cryptid who resembled a mossy tree come to life, piped up. "I heard you were flushed down into the fiery depths of the earth!"

"I heard you were blasted to the freezing top of the world!" The bellow came from Donald, an orange-furred, orangutan-like Bangladeshian Ban Manush.

A weaker voice, from the back of the crowd, awkwardly shouted, "No! I heard Chupacabra became the personal pet and crypto-servant to Señor Areck Gusto!"

A gasp burst from the creatures at the sound of this name. Some turned around to see who said it. Chupacabra peered over the heads of fur, scales, and feathers. He sniffed the air and scanned his audience.

In the back of the crowd, Eldon stared, horrified, at Jordan, who had his hands cupped over his mouth. They were both crouched down low. Then Jordan yelled out again. "It's true! Chupacabra became Gusto's lapdog! I even heard he fetched his slippers!"

As the shocked gasps turned silent, Jordan smiled at Eldon. "Hoax time," he whispered. "C'mon!" He led Eldon through the limbs and legs of the creatures, staying low as they made their way toward the stage.

Chupacabra stared out over the stunned, silent

cryptids. "So . . . I see you've all heard of Señor Areck Gusto! The powerful, terrifying human who tormented you all!" He stepped toward a box on the stage, allowing his skin of scales to sparkle in the sunlight. "Gusto! The horrible human who kidnapped the water cryptid and hijacked her Hydro-Hide!" Chupacabra lifted his club foot into the air. "The one who snatched a powerful Soil-Sole right off the earth cryptid's big foot!" Chupacabra reached into the box and lifted something out of it. He held it high above his head, like a professional wrestler holding up a championship belt.

It was Wilford's massive mustache.

"Gusto! Who recently swiped the great Yeti's abominable Blizzard-Bristles!" The crowd gasped again. Chupacabra held it high for all to see, then lowered it beneath his snout. An icy crackling was heard as the frosty inner hairs of the mustache attached themselves to Chupacabra's upper lip. He pulled his claws away and struck a pose, showing off his newest ill-gotten trophy.

"How did you get those?" a cryptid called out.

"By doing what your Creature Keepers could not do. I found Gusto and snatched back what he should never have been allowed to take. I did what we cryptids were born to do—hunt down any human who dares to take from us. You see, you do not need humans to protect you from me. You need me to protect you from humans. I know this because unlike all of you, I have survived in the world of humans, without the protection of the Creature Keepers. Only I understand the true threats that face us. And I say that the world will be dangerous for our kind only so long as it contains the human race!"

He twirled his new mustache and glanced up at something in the rafters. At the foot of the stage, Jordan and Eldon peered up as well. They could just make out Harvey Quisling hiding in the shadows. The old man held long handles attached to wires, like a puppeteer. Chupacabra nodded to him, then turned back to his audience.

"And I can do something the creature *captors* never bothered to do before they asked you to trust them. I will prove to you that I can protect you—by destroying before your very eyes the one human that even they couldn't stop from stealing the greatest powers from the greatest cryptids among us! I give you—*Señor Areck Gusto*!"

Quisling began to manipulate his puppet sticks up in the shadows, and Señor Areck Gusto awkwardly walked out onto the stage.

"You've got to be kidding," Eldon said. "That's the worst hoax I've ever seen."

"Looks like it's good enough to work on this crowd," Jordan said. The cryptids squawked and growled at the sight of the Gusto puppet. Its stuffed arms reached out clumsily as it stumbled toward them. They tried to shuffle backward, away from the stage. But Chupacabra silenced them.

"Stop! Look at you! You are the most magnificent, most powerful beings on the face of the earth, and yet you cower before a mere human! Watch and learn, my fellow cryptids—I will show you how we creatures deal with weak and puny men! Witness the power you hold inside each and every one of you!"

Chupacabra strutted up to Gusto and got in his face. "Gusto! You, like all humans, have tortured and ter-rorized my kind for long enough! Prepare to taste what all of your kind will soon know—*cryptid revenge!*"

Chupacabra reared up and lashed out at Gusto. His sharp claw flew toward the puppet's face—but the pup-pet ducked. *Whiff!* Chupacabra spun around, nearly falling over. The audience erupted. "*Ooooh!*"

Chupacabra regained his balance and glared at Gusto. The puppet stood still as a scarecrow. He leaped into the air, his Soil-Sole flying straight at the puppet's chest. At the last second, the puppet calmly took one step to its left.

CRASH! Chupacabra smashed into the solid stone sidewall of the amphitheater, his massive club foot blasting straight through it. Chupacabra angrily tried to pull his foot out of the wall as the Gusto puppet stepped up behind him, reached down, grabbed his tail, and yanked. Chupacabra went flying across the stage.

SMASH! The audience gasped as Gusto hit the opposite wall.

"I take it back," Eldon said to Jordan. "That's one heck of a puppet."

Enraged, Chupacabra pulled himself up off the floor, marched across the stage, and shot Harvey an angry look, then took a deep breath. He blew a wintry blast through his Blizzard-Bristles—not at the puppet but at its handler up in the rafters.

Harvey was hit with a sofa-sized snowball. It snapped the wires holding the puppet and sent the little puppeteer flying over the trees, landing somewhere in the jungle.

Chupacabra turned back and noticed the puppet wasn't where it should have been, lying lifelessly beneath its broken strings. In fact, it wasn't anywhere to be seen. Then Chupacabra felt a tap on his shoulder.

He spun around. Standing directly behind him was the Gusto puppet, grinning at him with its stitched-on pillowcase smile. Chupacabra lifted one of its arms and dropped it, letting it flop loosely at its side. He took the wire at the end of its sleeve and ran his fingers along it, following it down to the floor, where it connected to nothing.

WUMP! The Gusto puppet kicked Chupacabra so

hard in the tail, it sent him stumbling forward, falling flat on his newly mustached face and knocking his head against the stone wall.

All cryptid eyes were glued to the puppet as it lumbered forward, toward the front of the stage. It raised its arms and pulled its pillowcase head off its shoulders. The cryptids gasped, then fell silent, then broke out in a loud cheer. Standing there before them was the mysterious and legendary Yeti of the Himalayas. They rushed back toward the stage as Wilford tore off the rest of the Gusto clothing. As they cheered and howled, at the foot of the stage, Eldon smiled at Jordan. "Nice bit of hoaxing there, Elite Keeper Grimsley," he said.

The tone of the crowd shifted. Eldon and Jordan looked up. Onstage, Chupacabra had regained his wits and was charging toward Wilford. The Yeti spun around and grabbed hold of the Blizzard-Bristles, squeezing them together beneath Chupacabra's snout, just as the angry cryptid was taking a dangerously deep breath.

"Ah-ah," Wilford said. "I wouldn't do that if I were you. Sure, you'll blast me, but it'll also cause a blowback that will freeze you from the inside out, old friend."

Chupacabra slashed at the Yeti, knocking one of Wilford's paws away. Then he lifted his Soil-Sole and pressed it against Wilford's midsection. "That's the beauty of having more than one weapon," Chupacabra said. "You keep the element of surprise!"

THUD! He pushed off with his mighty foot, sending Wilford flying into the ancient stone back wall of the stage, which crumbled down on top of him. Chupacabra stumbled back, too, but regained his balance and slowly stood at the front of the stage to face the crowd, victorious.

There was a second of deadly silence. Then the entire cryptid audience burst out laughing. Chupacabra had half a mustache hanging under his right nostril, and he looked more than a little silly, even to this collection of odd creatures.

"How dare you laugh at me! I may not have destroyed Gusto, but I created him! And now I possess the stolen elemental powers! Do not think for a moment I won't hesitate to use them on any cryptid who refuses to follow me!"

"They do not wish to follow you," a voice boomed from behind him. Chupacabra spun around. Wilford stood atop the pile of rubble that had fallen on him. Hanging beneath his nose was the other half of his mustache, which looked much more natural on his face than on Chupacabra's. "Who would follow an old fool with half a mustache?"

Chupacabra felt under his snout, giving Wilford the upper hand—or in this case, the upper lip. Before the thieving cryptid could take another breath, Wilford blasted him through his half of the Blizzard-Bristles. A wash of snow slammed into Chupacabra, sending him tumbling off the front of the stage. The cryptids backed away, forming a circle around the thick, wet stream of white that viciously pummeled him. The concentrated squall pinned Chupacabra to the snow-covered ground.

Within seconds, it had mercilessly dumped what looked like a ton of snow on top of him in the center of the amphitheater field, sealing him beneath a freezing tomb of white.

A cheer of howls, growls, squeals, and snarls rose up from the cryptids as they circled in on the heaping snow pile in the center of the amphitheater field. Wilford hopped down off the stage and was met with backslapping and loud thanks and congratulations. Jordan rushed to join them.

"Great 'stache-slinging, Wilford!" Jordan exclaimed. "You got the drop on him!"

"Thank you," Wilford said. "That snowpack should hold. It was a real wet one."

Meanwhile, Eldon beelined toward the snow pile to keep the curious cryptids back. "Everyone, I need at least a twenty-foot perimeter!" He patrolled the field, keeping the cryptids away from even the wide apron of snow covering the ground all around the small white mountain.

Jordan stepped back and let out a deep breath. He finally felt he could breathe easy, for the first time in a long time. Looking around, he smiled at the celebratory mood that had suddenly entered the amphitheater. The scene had taken on the air of a family reunion. A weird one, in which everyone looked like they weren't from the same species—never mind the same family—but a reunion just the same. And if this was a big, weird family, Eldon looked happy in the role of its patriarch. Once the Badger Ranger had responsibly secured everyone's safety, he loosened up and started mingling. He knew every single cryptid by name. And now that the creatures weren't hypno-leashed with Chupacabra's homing device, they all recognized him, too. Jordan smiled as he watched. He knew how much this meant to Eldon.

Sandy, the Sumatran Golden Liger who'd ignored Eldon earlier, was standing with a few other cryptids. They were huddled close together, talking quietly, until Eldon approached. They suddenly broke up their huddle and stood stiffly, grinning at him awkwardly. Jordan noticed this and thought it seemed strange.

Eldon, of course, didn't notice. He put one arm around Sandy's neck and the other around Paul's (the Dingonek he'd been wrestling earlier). "Isn't this great, you guys? It's such a shame we can't get everyone together like this more often, but you know the Creature Keeper vow—help, hide, and hoax. I'm afraid it's just too risky!"

As Jordan looked on, his feeling that there was something odd going on grew stronger. Nothing dangerous or ominous, just *awkward*. It wasn't as if this small group of cryptids felt unhappy or upset, it just seemed like they felt . . . *guilty*. But of what?

"Don't worry," Eldon continued. "We'll all say our good-byes and have each of you back with your Keepers!" At this, the cryptids traded paranoid glances, signaling to Jordan that something odd was definitely going on. At the same time, another thought suddenly occurred him.

"*Keepers*." He glanced around. "Where are Abbie and Morris?" He broke away from the Yeti admirers and began frantically scanning the field. He spotted them on the opposite side of the grounds. Abbie and Morris were moving at a strangely slow but determinedly steady pace, straight toward the snow pile. Jordan could see by Abbie's worried expression that something was wrong. And Morris looked drowsy, almost as if— "Oh, no." Jordan spotted a murky green liquid sloshing around in Morris's bowl-head.

Jordan bolted toward them, weaving his way past groups of socializing cryptids. As he got closer, he could smell the valerian root. Horrible memories came rushing back from the last time that vile liquid came in contact with snow on the ground. And the two of them were nearly to the snow that surrounded the slope entombing Chupacabra.

"Abbie!" he cried out as he approached. "Abbie, stop!" She looked up at him but continued, determined to save Morris by replenishing his poisoned sara with the pure snow.

"Hey!" Eddie the Indonesian Ebu Gogo's voice suddenly cried out. "The snow pile is melting! It's turning all smushy!"

The massive white pile of packed snow began to sag and change shape. As it melted under the sun, it transformed into a great, big, bluish blob of slush. Cryptids panicked and stumbled away, cutting in front of Jordan and knocking him to the ground. Through the limbs and tails dashing before him, Jordan thought he spotted a ruby-red light, glowing deep within the base of the melting mountain. Then a split second later, the blob gave way, collapsing into an avalanche of watery ice.

Jordan helplessly turned toward Abbie and Morris, who were closest to the sloshy tsunami. She blocked the turtle cryptid's body with her own, bracing for the impact that was about to deep-freeze them both. Then, nothing happened.

The rapidly melting ice water suddenly gathered itself back up as if it were alive. It formed into a massive vertical tube, rising fifty feet above the snowy field. Jordan knew exactly what was happening. He'd seen this too many times before. It was one of Chupacabra's favorite Hydro-Hide tricks. His only thought was to get his sister out of danger.

As he ran toward her, the water arched over him like a giant tree bending in the wind, scooping Abbie and Morris high off the ground. It rose up again, balancing the two of them as it straightened into a pillar of water, towering above the amphitheater field.

Eldon and Wilford ran to Jordan's side. "It's Chupacabra!" Jordan shouted to them. "He's using his Hydro-Hide to manipulate the melted snow! We have to do something, or he could kill them both!"

Wilford quickly assessed the situation. He drew a deep breath and blew through his half of the Blizzard-Bristles. A fierce, arctic gust struck the base of the water pillar with a sharp *CRACK*, freezing it from the ground up. Inside the shaft of water, a blurred shadow

swam straight up the center, as Chupacabra raced against the freezing effect, staying just ahead of the ice, emerging at the top of the spout.

"It seems once again I have come out on top!" Chupacabra stood atop the ice tower beside Abbie and Morris, looking at the crowd below. He glanced at Abbie, then sniffed the air. He scanned the gathered cryptids below. Then he found who he was looking for. "I knew it! Old Georgie, beneath me as always!"

"Let them go!" Jordan yelled up to Chupacabra. "If it's me you want, come and get me! But those two have nothing to do with your plans!"

"Ah, but they do! Your granddaughter is my insurance policy! And the cryptid is my plan B! You see, that Mongolian Death Worm was useless once she finished digging those tunnels for me. I needed a fresh cryptid helper, one just as simpleminded and easily manipulated!"

Abbie was using all her strength to hold Morris steady, and all her concentration not to slip off the icy top of the newly frozen fountain. "You brainwashed them," she yelled. "You're a monster!" The turtle cryptid was swaying drowsily, and she held him tighter. "Morris! Stay awake, please!"

On the snow-covered ground, Wilford stepped forward. "All right, I've had quite enough of this overgrown mongrel. I put him up on that pedestal, and I can take him down."

"No, you can't!" Eldon exclaimed. "Morris's up there. And if he spills his sara before the last-quarter moon rises, he'll turn to stone, forever."

"Not to mention his sara is currently filled with that valerian-root juice," Jordan added. He pointed to the ground. "The second that stuff hits this snow, it vaporizes. Then it's nap time for everyone here. Remember what it did to your mountaintop?"

Wilford stepped back. The frightened cryptids panicked as they saw their hero couldn't help them. Some of them began to move toward the edges of the jungle. But Chupacabra stopped them in their tracks.

"No one move, or the Grimsley granddaughter is done for!" The cryptids turned and looked up. They all slowly began to shuffle back toward the center of the field.

Chupacabra sneered. "Just as I suspected. You're pathetic, all of you! You actually *care* about these humans! I see now that you'll never join with me willingly. So be it. Your choice will be made for you, and for your own good. Time for plan B."

The cryptids gasped as Chupacabra reached out and put his claw around Abbie's neck. He looked at Morris with his glowing red eyes. "Now, my dim-witted little friend, you're going to step off this platform and drop to the snowy ground below. Think you can handle that?"

"No!" Abbie could feel his sharp claw against her neck. "He'll die!"

"For a good cause. There's enough liquefied valerian-root powder in that empty head of his to put that entire crowd into a lovely stupor. I've given those crypto-sheep every opportunity to join me and rise against the humans of their own free will."

Jordan, Eldon, Wilford, and the others stared up in silence, helpless to do anything. Eldon stepped forward. "Don't be a monster, Chupacabra! Let her go! It's me you want revenge against—I'm the leader of the Creature Keepers! Make an example of me to win them over! You can't get your way by controlling their minds!"

He snarled back at Eldon. "You call me a monster for controlling their minds? It's you and your Creature Keepers who brainwashed them, long ago, to hide themselves from the world, to cower in the shadows like they should be ashamed of their magnificence. I'm just fixing a broken system, by any means necessary!" He turned and smiled at Morris, and spoke in a sly, soothing voice. "It's all right, my friend. You're just going to help me put them all to sleep, in order to wake them up, don't you see? It's time we all wake up and stop following these pathetic humans. Come, now. I need you to take this one small step for a cryptid, but one giant leap for cryptid-kind."

Morris's big eyes were locked on Abbie's. She recognized and remembered his expression. It was the same look of fear and confusion as the day they first met, when he was torn between leaving the river and coming with her.

"Master? What do I do?"

"No human is your master," Chupacabra suddenly snapped. "I am! And I would push you off this platform if I could! I cannot kill you, but I can kill her! Is this getting through that thick-shelled skull of yours? Now I command you to jump, or she will die!"

"Listen to me, Morris," Abbie said softly. "He can't push you off, because he can't kill another creature. You need to think for yourself, now. You need to be your own master. I thought you were the special one with a rare power. I still believe you have something special inside you, Morris. You have the power of a good and pure heart. Choose now. Do what you know is right. Use your power."

"Enough!" Chupacabra yelled. "Jump now, or the girl dies!"

Abbie smiled through her tears. "It's okay, Morris. Whatever he does to me is okay." Morris smiled back at her. "As you wish"—he turned his gaze to Chupacabra—"my new master."

"What?" Abbie's eyes grew wide. "Morris, no!"

"Silence!" Chupacabra's grip tightened on her neck, and he put his other claw over her mouth. "This cryptid is smarter than he looks. And he's made his choice! Now take that step and show everyone who your true master is. Oh, and how about a cannonball. I do love a good cannonball."

"Of course. But first, I must bow to my new master. It is tradition."

Abbie's eyes grew wide. She squealed under Chupacabra's claw. "Excellent," Chupacabra sneered. "At last, some respect!"

Morris stepped back, closed his eyes, and quickly lowered his head. The murky green valerian-root liquid came splashing out of his sara, onto the ice platform at Chupacabra's feet. It burst into a thick plume of green fog as it hit the ice, engulfing them.

"YOU HALF-WIT!" Chupacabra shrieked. He released Abbie and pushed against Morris. He tried to leap up from the toxic gas but was yanked back violently. His tail was submerged in the ice tower. He hadn't made it all the way out the top when it froze, and now he was leashed to the rising cloud of noxious green gas. Chupacabra fell to his knees as he choked on the heavy gas, overcome with the thick green plume. From the ground, Jordan caught a glimpse of something small and red, like a gemstone, pop out of Chupacabra's claw. It bounced off the ice and sailed out of view.

Morris grabbed Abbie as he fell backward, pulling her tightly to his body before plummeting away from the tower of noxious gas and toward the snowy ground—in a perfect cannonball.

31

*B*OOM! Morris hit the ground shell-first, with the impact of a meteorite. Dirt and snow exploded as he slammed heavily into the earth. Jordan, Eldon, Wilford, and the cryptids began to rush toward the crater, until they heard a horrible sound from above.

KERRRRACCCKK! Massive splits shot down the ice tower. Through the fog at the top, Jordan could make out a woozy Chupacabra, lying on his back, weakly lifting his Soil-Sole, stomping on the ice, and breaking it into shards.

KRACK! One last stomp caused the tower to splinter. Everyone on the ground ran for cover as sharp shards of ice came crashing down. In the center of it all, just as he had risen, Chupacabra plummeted through the shaft of falling ice. His limp body hit the ground, followed by a cross-hatching of giant ice spears that completely buried him.

As the pile of ice settled, an odor filled the chilly air. The thick plume of valerian-root gas seeped out from the ice tomb that had buried Chupacabra, spreading across the field, reaching out into the crowd of cryptids.

"The gas!" Eldon said. "Everyone move back!"

The cryptids panicked, pushing and shoving, slithering and creeping over one another as they backed away toward the outer edges of the clearing, closer to the jungle tree line. Those overcome with the gas began to stumble and pass out. Others were coughing and choking.

Jordan, Eldon, and Wilford tried to avoid breathing the toxic fog as they split up to help the others. Jordan needed to reach Abbie and Morris. Eldon was intent on getting to the cryptids who were overcome with the nauseous gas. And Wilford was working his way toward the pile of ice that had entombed the poisoned Chupacabra.

As the gas caught more cryptids trying to escape, Jordan pressed on, avoiding it as best he could. But it was everywhere, and he felt his legs get heavier as he

made his way toward the crater where Morris and his sister had crash-landed. The green mist was overtaking him, and his vision was growing blurrier by the second.

Thup-thup-thup-thup! A noise accompanied the sensation of something wet and warm hitting his face. It was a thick, gooey orange liquid, raining down over the amphitheater. Jordan felt his sleepiness lift as the green fog began to dissolve.

Thup-thup-thup-thup! What was left of the haze swirled up and away like it was being vacuumed up. As it cleared, Jordan could make out a welcome sight. The Heli-Jet hovered low over the field, with Bernard and Zaya in the cockpit window. Not only were they clearing the air with the repaired rotors, they also had a secret weapon: strapped to the bottom of the Heli-Jet was the Mongolian Death Worm, spitting out the orange goo—what must have been valerian-root antidote—all over the crowd.

"It's Corky!" Jordan yelled, his senses sharpening as he shook off the drowsy effect of the gas. He never thought he'd be so happy to see a giant Death Worm.

The bulbous cryptid waved her tail as she happily spit out the syrupy cure, spraying the entire scene with her warm, medicinal regurgitation. Bernard dropped

Corky onto the field, then set the Heli-Jet down. Jagger and the other monks leaped out of the side cargo door armed with apple juice cartons filled with the antidote and ran to the cryptids lying unconscious, while the Mongolian Death Worm continued happily spitting directly in the faces of others in need.

With both the air and his head now clearing, Jordan was finally able to reach the hole where Morris had landed. "Abbie!" He shouted into it. "Are you all right?" All he could see was the side of Morris's shell. A horrible feeling overtook him as he reached down and touched it. It was cold. And solid. The cryptid had turned to stone. There was a sniffling from beneath it. Jordan leaned farther into the crater and saw Abbie, completely unscratched and protected, still wrapped in Morris's solid stone arms. She looked up at her brother with tears in her eyes. "I couldn't save him," she said. "So he saved me."

As Eldon and the cryptids gathered silently behind him, Jordan reached down and gently pulled his sister free from the stone embrace that saved her life. Wilford helped them out of the crater. Then they all stared down at the lifeless statue that was Morris.

"We can't leave him here," Abbie said. "We're taking him home."

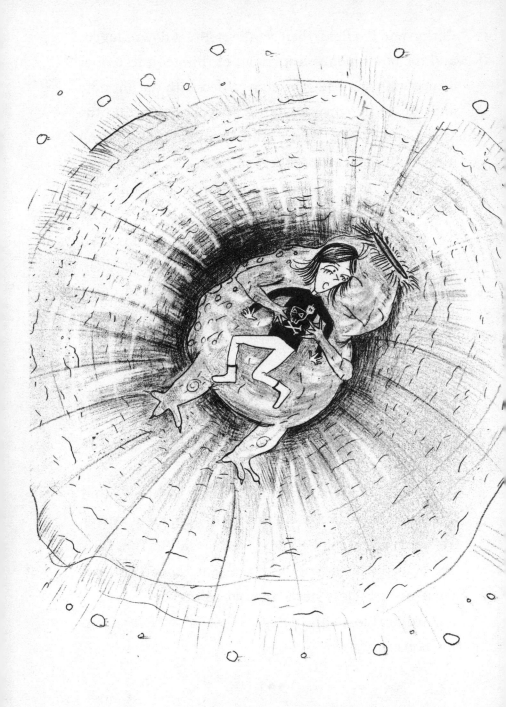

As the sun dipped below the tree line, Jordan, Eldon, Wilford, and the others organized all the cryptids to help pull Morris from his tomb. Zaya sat with Abbie, trying his best to comfort her. Behind them, Corky cooed and purred as Zaya stroked her belly. Abbie smiled through her sadness and patted the Death Worm. Corky purred louder. "Hey, I think she might actually like you," Zaya said with a gentle smile.

"That's nice," Abbie said. "I could use a new friend right now."

"Oh. Uh, I was talking to Corky."

Abbie laughed despite herself, and Zaya chuckled as he put his arm around her.

As the other cryptids dug a wider trench to better remove Morris, Jordan, Eldon, Bernard, and Wilford approached the pile of ice left from the tower. Somewhere deep inside the crisscrossing, beam-like shards lay Chupacabra.

"We got him," Eldon said. "But now we've got to find a way to keep him."

"What do we do when he wakes up?" Bernard asked.

"*If* he wakes up," Jordan said. "He inhaled a lot of that gas before he fell."

"He will not revive," Wilford said. "But not because of the gas. Chupacabra ended the life of another cryptid.

His fate is now tied to that which he ended. With or without the gas and the ice, he's forever frozen, just like the Kappa he pushed off that tower."

"That's good," Bernard said. "Then we can just crack the ice open and take back Nessie's Hydro-Hide, Syd's Soil-Sole, and Wilford's Blizzard-Bristle, right?"

"I wouldn't be too sure," Eldon said. "Because Morris turned to stone, we don't know if he was in fact killed. He may be only frozen forever. Either way he can never be revived, and that's a very sad thing. But until we know for certain that Chupacabra is dead in there, we need to be extremely cautious. It might be safer to get him somewhere we can carefully extract what he stole. Unless, of course, any of you are feeling lucky."

They studied the ice pile that contained Chupacabra. No one was in the mood to take any chances. Wilford drew a deep breath and blew through his half Blizzard-Bristle. A smooth, thick layer of ice sealed the cage of crisscrossing shards, suspending Chupacabra in a frozen, igloo-shaped cage. "Safe for travel," Wilford said.

Jordan smiled up at him. "Fro-yurt," he said. The Yeti smiled back.

"I'm thinking the new chamber Peggy and I carved beneath your grandfather's house would make a very nice temperature-controlled laboratory where we could take our time as well as every precaution," Eldon said to Jordan. He turned to Wilford. "But until good ol' C. E. Noodlepen makes a withdrawal of funds for the equipment that will require, do you think we might store him up on one of the five treasures of the high snow? I know you have room, and for now, the colder he is, the better."

"You all know how much I love having guests," Wilford joked. "The monks will keep a sharp eye on him, while I keep an icy wind on him, twenty-four hours a day, just to be safe."

Jordan turned to follow the others, when something on the ground caught his eye. Glimmering beneath a chunk of ice was a small ruby-red stone. He crouched, picked it up, and put it in his pocket.

It took the strength of all the cryptids pulling together, a rocket-enhanced Heli-Jet, a giant Mongolian Death Worm, and a handful of mountain monks to lift Morris's heavy stone body out of the crater. Then, with Wilford laying down a slick path of ice through the lush forest of Medog, they eventually were able to slide Morris to the hard-packed, snowy crater walls surrounding it. Trailing behind the procession, Jordan, Abbie, and Eldon pushed the igloo-shaped ice cage that held Chupacabra along the same glide path.

It was hours later when they all gathered in the dark before the entrances to the tunnels. One by one, the wandering cryptids silently paid their respects to the brave little creature. Jordan then checked each of their GCPS collars to be sure they were all back in working order now that Syd's CHUPA-enhanced homing collar had been destroyed. Then the creatures were sent off through their appropriate tunnels for the journey back to their respective Creature Keeper.

Sandy, Paul, and the rest of the group of cryptids Jordan had noticed acting strangely earlier were at it again. After paying their respects to Morris, they huddled together and seemed to be discussing something important. Eldon noticed, too. He and Jordan approached them.

"I know it's tough, guys," Eldon said. "But you need to say your good-byes and start heading home."

"We know," Paul said. "And we are saying good-bye. But not to one another. To you. To the Creature Keepers."

"We're out," Donald said, holding out his red-furred hand and nodding toward the ice cage. "That kooky dude was dead wrong about nearly everything, but something he said rang true. We don't need to be kept. We need to be free." The red-furred Bangladeshi Ban Manush dropped his GCPS collar into Eldon's hand. "But thanks for everything."

Eldon was speechless. "Wait," Jordan said. "You

guys need to think about this. You don't know what it's like out in the world."

"That's kind of the point," Francine said bluntly. She handed Eldon her collar as well.

"Unacceptable!" Eldon said. "You put these back on and you march right back to your Keepers, do you understand me?"

Sandy the Golden Liger was the last to step forward. "It's not you, Eldon," she said. "It's us. We do love you. And we love our Keepers. This is not an easy decision for us. But it's the right one. What Morris did up there of his own free will, for all of us, was our final inspiration. He can't have sacrificed for us just so we could all go back to living in the shadows. It's time we do as he did, and choose to live our own lives." She tore her collar off and dropped it at Eldon's feet. "Good-bye for now, old friend."

Eldon and Jordan stood awestruck as the pack of cryptids walked together toward a far tunnel entrance. They glanced at one another, then entered it, disappearing into the darkness together. They never looked back.

Bernard approached. "Hey, where are *they* going?"

Eldon was at a loss for words again. He crouched down and picked up Sandy's collar. Jordan spoke up for him. "Wherever they want, I guess."

Bernard stared at the tunnel entrance and watched as the gold light faded away.

Zaya had attached one end of a long, heavy chain he'd gotten off the Heli-Jet to Corky's tail. The other end he'd secured around Morris. Eldon studied his Badger Ranger pocket compass and wandered a little ways from the tunnel openings. He stopped at an untouched area of the wall of snow. "Here," he said. "Due east."

Jordan and Abbie drew a large X on the snowbank as Zaya led Corky toward it. Wilford pushed from behind, and soon this bizarre-looking caravan was aimed at the X-mark in the white wall.

Bernard and the monks approached them. "Okay," the Skunk Ape said. "We've got Chupacabra loaded up and secured on the Heli-Jet, all set to go."

"Thank you," Eldon said. "You understand what we need you to do?"

"Of course. I'll deliver them all to Mount Kanchenjunga, safe and sound."

Wilford bent down to speak to the monks. "I will help return Morris to his home. I need to ask you guys to babysit a frosty old cryptid at the top of a cold, lonely mountain. Do you think you can do that for me?"

Jagger giggled. "Yeah. I think we can handle that."

Bernard gave Morris a final, tearful hug, then said his good-byes to Abbie and Zaya, who were feeding Corky some nutritious jungle fruit. Lastly, he approached Jordan and Eldon. "Thanks, Bernard." Jordan smiled. "You went beyond the call of duty."

"My pleasure," Bernard said. "And speaking of, I was thinking after I drop the monks off and see that Chupacabra is guarded in a safe spot, I might swoop down and try to find the other end of the tunnel those guys went down on their own."

"You'll do no such thing," Eldon said. Jordan glanced at him, surprised. This was the most short-tempered he could recall hearing Eldon speak to his creature. "I need you back at the central command, do you understand?"

"But as a cryptid I might be able to persuade them to—"

"*Bernard!*" Everyone looked over as Eldon snapped. The Badger Ranger took a deep breath, then spoke in a calmer but still very tense tone. "You have your orders. Fly them back to Mount Kanchenjunga, then return to base. Are we clear?"

Bernard looked at Eldon with an expression of hurt and anger. "Yes, *sir*," he said. He turned and stormed toward the Heli-Jet, the mountain monks in tow.

"I'm sorry I lost my temper," Eldon said to Jordan.

"I don't think it's me you should apologize to."

"He'll understand," Eldon said. "I'll make it up to him when we're all home. He's had his eye on a pair of roller skates." Eldon trudged over to Corky and the others. Jordan watched Bernard make his way toward the Heli-Jet, and ran to catch up to him.

"Bernard," he said. "Listen, he didn't mean it. He's just really upset. He's never had a cryptid leave the CK before, and you know how he likes his rules—"

"It's fine," the Skunk Ape said coldly. "Forget it."

Jordan stepped in front of Bernard. He was clearly hurt and embarrassed. For all his good-mannered helpfulness, Bernard really was a sensitive creature.

Jordan glanced over at Eldon, who was busy with his compass near Abbie, Zaya, and Corky. "Listen," he whispered. "After you drop them off at Kanchenjunga, why don't you take a day or so and, y'know, *unwind*."

"Unwind?"

Jordan glanced over again. "Yeah. Maybe fly down to the lower Himalayas, see the sights." He winked at Bernard. "We won't be back from Japan for a few days. No one needs to know. I'll see to that. Besides, you earned it."

A grin spread over Bernard's face. "Thank you, Jordan." He lifted him up, gave him a great big skunky hug, then set him down. "Travel safely, now."

Jordan smiled up at his old friend. "You too, Bernard."

Wilford, Zaya, and Eldon were working at the front end of Corky, leading her to the large *X* drawn on the eastern face of the snow crater. At her opposite end, Abbie stood next to the solidified Morris. Jordan approached her cautiously.

"If I only could've protected him one more night," she said, staring skyward.

Jordan looked up. Surrounded by thousands of stars was the quarter moon, shaped like a perfect white turtle shell floating in the night sky.

"C'mon, Ab," Jordan said. "Let's take him home."

"Okay, girl," Zaya said into the side of his Mongolian Death Worm. "Chow time!"

Corky opened her gaping mouth and took a massive bite out of the snow wall. She took another, then another. As she began to wriggle forward into her own tunnel, she pulled the long chain, and Morris followed. Wilford helped tug the chain while blowing through his half Blizzard-Bristles between Corky and Morris, creating a track of slick ice on the tunnel floor. As Jordan, Abbie, Eldon, and Zaya pushed from behind, the statue began to slide along steadily.

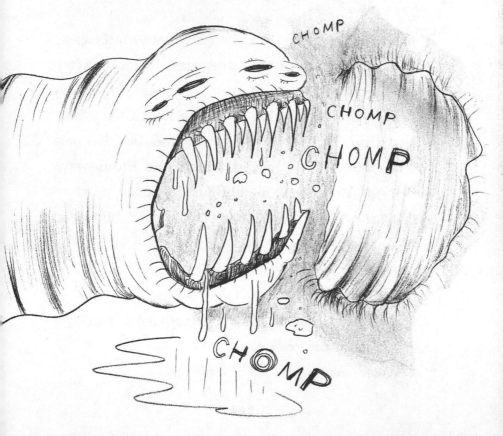

The tunnel trek beneath the snowbound landscape of central China was long and very difficult. After days of making their way, they finally emerged from the deep snow at the banks of the East China Sea, where they were met by Nessie and her Keeper, Alistair MacAlister. Jordan, Abbie, and Eldon were elated to see them, and not just because Alistair greeted them with a submarine full of food, blankets, and supplies.

"Thank goodness you found your way out of the ice," Jordan said.

"Aye," Alistair said. "Haggis-Breath led us through, and just in the nick of time."

"Were you running out of air?"

"Aye, *fresh* air. It was getting a wee bit ripe down in that sub."

Now that they were out of the long, cold tunnel, they spotted signs that the continent Chupacabra had cruelly transformed into a snowy wasteland was slowly beginning to thaw. Even the frozen East China Sea had begun to split into large, thick chunks of ice. Alistair brought the travelers up to speed on the aftermath of Chupacabra's great blizzard.

"The human world in these parts all pretty much stayed indoors and hunkered down, which was probably for the best. We're lucky nobody got seriously hurt by the storm. To them it was just a one-in-a-century freak blizzard. So that's good." Alistair glanced past them and gazed upon Morris. "'Course, I wish we could say that about our crew."

Abbie hadn't spoken for nearly the entire journey. But she spoke up now. "Alistair, where's Kriss?"

"He flew Katsu and Shika home from here," Alistair said. "The twins wanted to prepare for the little guy's final arrival."

They all worked together to slide Morris onto one of the massive floating ice blocks and prepared for the final leg of their journey back to his home. The only ones who didn't join them on the iceberg were Zaya and Corky.

"I'm afraid this is where we must leave you," Zaya said softly. Corky, exhausted from tunneling and dragging Morris, snored beside him. "Please give Katsu and Shika my deepest sympathies. Tell them I had to tend to my creature."

"I'm sure they'll understand," Jordan said. He took off his Elite Keeper badge. "I'd like to give this to Corky, for her incredible strength in proving who she really was. Also, some top-notch spitting." He took a look at the massive sleeping worm, then decided to place the pin in Zaya's hand, remembering what happened when Eldon woke her. "I'll let you do the honors, when you get home."

Corky opened a sleepy eye and spotted Jordan. Her humongous mouth stretched into a wide grin—and sprayed Jordan's face with regurgitated snow-slush. Then she licked it off with her long, forked tongue.

"She doesn't do that to everyone," Zaya said. "She may have a crush on you."

"Wow," Jordan said, wiping off the warm, wet slobber. "I'm flattered."

Zaya smiled as Abbie approached. She removed her pin and attached it to the Creature Keeper's shirt. "This one's for you," she said. "For being a great Keeper and a good friend. And not just to Corky." She kissed him on the cheek. He blushed and nodded his thanks.

The others said their good-byes to Zaya and Corky, and the two of them tunneled off beneath the snow in the direction of the Mongolian Desert.

Jordan, Abbie, Eldon, and Wilford stepped onto the glacier with Morris. Alistair and Nessie provided the final push across the icy sea toward Japan, all the way back to Morris's riverside home in the great beech-tree forest.

As they floated toward the mainland, Jordan noticed Eldon standing at the edge of the small iceberg, staring across the cold, dark water.

"I know you're worried about those cryptids," Jordan said. "I'm sure they'll be all right. Maybe this is just another step in a new direction. For all of us."

"Maybe," Eldon said. "But it's not a step I'm ready to take with you."

He held his hand out and dropped something into Jordan's palm. Jordan lifted the clear, crystal ring that had belonged to his grandfather. Inside it, the liquid swirled and sparkled. It reminded Jordan of the stars atop Mount Kanchenjunga.

"Jordan, I leave you and your sister in charge of the Creature Keepers."

"Are you sure?"

"I made a promise to your grandfather that I'd take care of his organization, and I did the best I could to keep my word. But you're right. Things are changing, and I am not the person to lead us through those changes. Chupacabra is defeated, so I leave you both with a fresh, blank page. You are George Grimsley's grandchildren. You are the rightful heirs to this responsibility. And you're ready." He stared out at the dark sea. "Besides, I feel like I'm getting too old for this stuff."

"What will you do?"

Eldon shrugged. "Keep getting older, I suppose."

Jordan studied Eldon's face. In the moonlight, he could see the hurt and pain that those cryptids leaving his protection had caused. It made him look older, and tired.

"But you got sick before, and this ring made you all better."

Eldon smiled. "The restorative powers of that ring can do amazing things. You and your sister may need it for more important things than keeping me from getting the sniffles."

"All right," Jordan said. "If it's what you really want, Abbie and I will be honored to carry on not only our grandfather's legacy, but yours, as well." Eldon looked at him, and Jordan slipped the ring on his finger. "But we've got Chupacabra frozen in ice, a lab to build back in Florida, and quite possibly an

undiscovered fourth special cryptid out there somewhere. I'm thinking we may still need some good ol'
Badger Ranger know-how."

Eldon smiled and saluted his friend. "It'd be a Badger Ranger's honor," he said.

Nessie stayed behind to guard the submarine just offshore as the others made the final push across the icy
ground into Morris's home. The trees and forest floor
were blanketed with snow, giving the cryptid's riverside neighborhood an empty, lonely feeling. It was the
same feeling Jordan and Abbie shared as they helped
deliver Morris to his Keepers, who were waiting near

the side of the Anmon River to see him.

Abbie took a deep, unsteady breath as she approached Katsu and Shika. She began by bowing to them, then she spoke softly. "I want you both to know that I tried my best to protect him. But I know you can never forgive me. I don't think I can ever forgive myself. I loved Morris, and I'll never forget him."

Katsu glared at her, as sternly as the day they first met back on the doorstep of Eternal Acres. Then, oddly, he bowed to her. "There is nothing for which to forgive," he said. "We heard how Morris sacrificed himself to save his friends. We are sad and we will miss him, but we are very proud of him."

Shika had tears in her eyes, but she smiled as she took Abbie's hands. "And I am also proud of my BFF," she said. "You brought our Kappa out into the world. You helped him realize that he is his own master. For that, we thank you."

"I don't know what to say," Abbie said. "I didn't do any of those things."

"Yes, you did," Katsu added. "We never should have left him in his stone state like we did. We thought it was the safest thing to do. But sometimes the safest thing is not always the best thing. You brought him to life. More than that, you brought him out of his shell."

Abbie hadn't smiled in days, and suddenly she felt an

uncontrollable giggle coming on. It might have been the exhaustion, or Katsu's accidental joke, or some combination. "I'm sorry," she said. "It's not funny, it's just . . . he said—" Abbie was suddenly overcome with laughter. Shika gave her a strange look, then glanced at her brother. Katsu was smiling, too. He began to giggle. Then he burst out with a high-pitched howl. That's when Shika broke out in a surprisingly snorting chuckle. Soon everyone was laughing. Wilford let out a deep, echoing belly laugh, almost as loud as Alistair MacAlister's. A snicker from the shadows turned Abbie's head. Standing there, giggling softly, was Kriss. She smiled at the Mothman, and the sight of him made her feel much better. Everyone was so tired after their long, sober journeys, and so emotionally drained from their adventures, that they couldn't seem to stop themselves—soon they all fell down in hysterics around Morris's stone feet. Abbie took a last look at Morris and couldn't help but feel the solid stone cryptid was smiling down on them. She smiled back as everyone's laughter filled the forest, rising through the cold air, helping to thaw the frosty trees.

Alistair and Kriss built a small campfire in front of Morris. Shika made an herbal tea from a blend of plants she plucked from beneath the thawing snow, while Katsu prepared a few extra beds in the teak and bamboo teahouse hidden in the trees near the river.

They all settled around the fire, where Jordan and Abbie shared tales of Morris's adventures. Katsu and Shika laughed and gasped at the amazing stories. The twin Creature Keepers couldn't believe all the incredible things their little cryptid had done.

Later, once Eldon, Alistair, and the twins had made their way to the teahouse to sleep and Wilford had ambled off to a bed of snow he'd gathered up in the nearby forest, Abbie and Kriss went off to sit near the riverside. Jordan watched as she rested her head on Kriss's furry shoulder. After a moment, the two of them stood, and Jordan quietly approached. Kriss gave Abbie a gentle hug, then glanced shyly at Jordan. He flapped his wings and shot straight up into the air, settling into a perch high atop a beech tree.

"Sorry," Jordan said, looking up. "I didn't mean to interrupt anything."

"It's okay," Abbie said. "We're just friends. He's a good listener, that's all."

"Oh," Jordan said, secretly relieved that his sister wasn't dating a Mothman. "Well, I know I'm just your little brother, but I can listen pretty good, too, y'know. Maybe not as good as a cryptid who barely ever even whispers—but if you ever need, y'know, like a *human* to listen to you—"

"Shut up, dorkface." She flashed a smile at him,

then crouched down by the icy river. "This is the exact spot where I first filled him up. The first time he—" Her voice quavered a little. "I mean, it wasn't like the second time, when he just popped out of the bay all fresh and new. The first time, I saw it with my own eyes. He came back to life, right in front of me." She turned and looked over at Morris, standing motionless by the dwindling fire. "Right where he's standing now."

Abbie reached down. Her hands broke through the thin layer of ice and entered the chilly water gurgling beneath. She made a bowl with her hands, scooped water from the river, and stood up.

"Abbie, don't," Jordan said, following her toward Morris. "You know it won't work."

"I know," she said. "It's not for him. It's for me."

She lifted her hands and let the cold water trickle through her fingers into Morris's sara. She stepped back. Abbie and Jordan stared into Morris's stone face for a good, long time.

"It's late," Jordan finally said softly. "Maybe we should get some rest."

"I hate leaving him out here all alone," Abbie turned to face her brother. "I wish you were right about Grampa Grimsley. I wish our grandfather *was* still alive. He could come sit with Morris and keep him company like he used to, counting the stars with him until he drifted off to sleep." As she looked up at the starry sky through the trees, Jordan felt his grandfather's ring on his finger.

Abbie leaned in and kissed Morris's cold stone beak. "You're still the most special creature I've ever known. And I'll miss you. Good night, Morris."

She shuffled off through the snow, toward the teahouse. Jordan watched her go, then looked back at the stone face before him. He remembered Morris's stories of Grampa Grimsley, his first and oldest friend. Jordan pulled the ring off his finger.

"This was his," Jordan said to the motionless turtle face. "Why don't you hold on to it tonight. Maybe it'll help you to find him, wherever the two of you are now." He tried to place it on Morris's thick stone finger, but it wouldn't fit. He reached up and dropped it into the river water in Morris's sara.

"At the very least, I hope it helps you sleep in peace tonight." Jordan smiled at the Kappa one last time, then turned and went off to bed.

The next morning, a loud splashing woke Jordan from a dead sleep. He rubbed his eyes and sat up in the little cot Shika had set up for him. He looked around the teahouse. Both the twins and Alistair were still asleep, but Abbie wasn't in her cot. He turned and shook Eldon. "Hey," he said. "Wake up! Abbie's gone! And I think I heard something. C'mon!"

The two of them stepped out of the teahouse and were immediately surprised by their surroundings. The forest had completely thawed. The Anmon River was no longer frozen, and its water was rushing loudly along its banks. The snow had melted, and the runoff had swollen the river near to the point of overflowing. The snow and ice from the beech trees dripped from its sagging branches like rain, and the ground was slushy and wet. It was as if spring had sprung overnight.

They walked across the muddy ground looking for Abbie. As they approached the place where they'd sat the night before, Jordan thought they had the wrong campfire. The soggy embers were exactly where they were supposed to be, but something was missing. Morris was gone.

Jordan and Eldon shared a look. Then they glanced down. There on the ground in the mud and slush were two pairs of footprints. One human, and one—

"It can't be," Eldon said.

Jordan and Eldon burst into a sprint, running along the riverbank, following the footprints. There was no need for spooring techniques now—these were fresh and easy to follow. The noisy river grew louder as its wild current splashed and sloshed against its banks. They stopped at a spot where the tracks suddenly disappeared into the water. There was another splash, followed by laughter.

Abbie stood all alone in the center of a tranquil pool created by large rocks blocking the current. There were tears in her eyes—and a huge grin. Suddenly, something large burst from beneath the surface. It spun in the air and landed in the water before bobbing back up again. There, floating on his back, happily spouting water into the air, was Morris—alive as ever.

"Morris!" a voice called from behind Jordan and Eldon.

"You're alive!" another voice cried out.

Shika and Katsu ran past the two boys and dived into the river, swimming toward the delighted cryptid. When they reached him, they happily hugged and splashed in the water. Abbie stood back and smiled at them. Kriss swooped down and sat on one of the rocks, and she and the Mothman shared a grin.

Onshore, a winded Alistair limped up beside Jordan and Eldon. "Well, I'll be a salamander's soggy patootie," he said, staring out at the spectacle in the pool.

A deep Yeti chuckle echoed through the forest as Wilford lumbered up to the scene. "Wilford," Jordan said. "How could this happen? How could he come back?"

"I do not know." A smile crept out from behind the Yeti's half mustache. "And it is not my concern." He took two great strides, and leaped into the pool—a perfect cannonball. A massive flume of water shot high into the air.

"Yahoo!" Alistair ran and dived in behind him, belly flopping into the river.

"I don't understand this," Eldon said. "His sara emptied three times between the first-quarter moons.

He should have turned to stone, permanently." He looked at Jordan. "The *Raising and Caring for Your Kappa* guidebook is very clear on this rule."

"Maybe some of those old rules are changing, too." Jordan burst out laughing as he dived into the water with the others.

Eldon smiled as he watched everyone splashing around with Morris. They all turned and egged him to come in. The First-Class Badger Ranger methodically removed his regulation Badger Ranger boots, followed by his thick, woolly socks, laying them neatly on a dry rock. He stepped into the cold water, and stopped.

As the others splashed and swam, Eldon Pecone took a step to join them, when something caught his eye. Glimmering beneath the water's surface was George Grimsley's ring. He crouched, picked it up, and put it in his pocket. Then he dived into the Anmon River, joining his friends in the swirling, crystal-clear pool.

The water was freezing cold, but none of them seemed to notice. And if they did, they didn't seem to be the least bit concerned.